TESTED LOVE

A CHRISTIAN ROMANCE

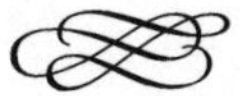

JULIETTE DUNCAN

BOOK 2 "THE TRUE LOVE SERIES"

COPYRIGHT

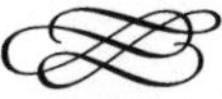

NOTE: This book asset in Australia, and therefore Australian spelling, terminology, and phrasing have been used throughout.

PRAISE FOR "TESTED LOVE"

"Ben & Tessa's story is continued in this book and their love is truly tested. As with many blended families there are ups and downs as the family members work to be a unified group. Juliette's writing continues to be so realistic that I felt like I was right there in the midst of the stories." *Charlotte*

"Wow, this book covers many of the problems of a new marriage with the husband having a wounded teen age son, true to life, we know. But very clearly, we are instructed how to trust God with all vs. going into deep depression or giving up, blaming God! Good lesson in all the books." *Butterfly*

"A very true to life story that gives wonderful insight into the difficulties of divorce and teenage children struggling with it. Godly and insightful Juliette's books keep reminding me of God's goodness in all situations." *Reader*

"I thoroughly enjoy immersing myself in the lives of these characters." *Elenna*

ALSO BY JULIETTE DUNCAN

Find all of Juliette Duncan's books on her website: www.julietteduncan.com/library

True Love Series

Tender Love

Tested Love

Tormented Love

Triumphant Love

Precious Love Series

Forever Cherished

Forever Faithful

Forever His

Water's Edge Series

When I Met You

Because of You

With You Beside Me

All I Want is You

It Was Always You

My Heart Belongs to You

A Sunburned Land Series

A mature-age romance series

Slow Road to Love

Slow Path to Peace

Slow Ride Home

Slow Dance at Dusk

Slow Trek to Triumph

Christmas at Goddard Downs

The Shadows Series

A jilted teacher, a charming Irishman, & the chance to escape their pasts & start again.

Lingering Shadows

Facing the Shadows

Beyond the Shadows

Secrets and Sacrifice

A Highland Christmas

A Time For Everything Series

A mature-age Christian Romance series

A Time to Treasure

A Time to Care

A Time to Abide

A Time to Rejoice

Transformed by Love Christian Romance Series

Because We Loved

Because We Forgave

Because We Dreamed

Because We Believed

Because We Cared

Billionaires with Heart Series

Her Kind-Hearted Billionaire

Her Generous Billionaire

Her Disgraced Billionaire

Her Compassionate Billionaire

The Potter's House Books...

Stories of hope, redemption, and second chances.

The Homecoming

Unchained

Blessings of Love

The Hope We Share

The Love Abounds

Love's Healing Touch

Melody of Love

Whispers of Hope

Promise of Peace

Heroes Of Eastbrooke Christian Suspense Series

Safe in His Arms

Under His Watch

Within His Sight

Freed by His Love

Stand Alone Christian Romantic Suspense

Leave Before He Kills You

The Madeleine Richards Series

Although the 3 book series is intended mainly for pre-teen/Middle Grade girls, it's been read and enjoyed by people of all ages.

CHAPTER 1

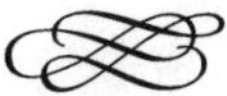

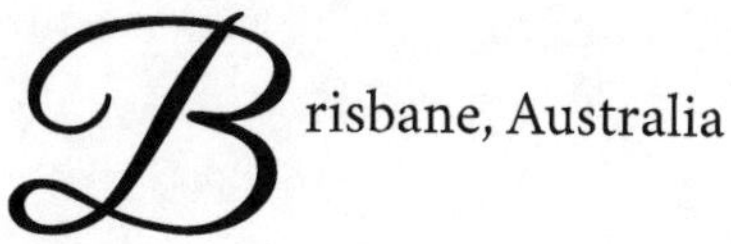risbane, Australia

TESSA WILLIAMS SLIPPED her arm through her husband's as the newlyweds stood on the pavement gazing at the house they were about to call home. "I'm so glad we chose this house, Ben. I absolutely love it!"

Both the architect and builder had done a great job of creating the modern sleek family home, blending it into the surrounding neighbourhood of New Farm, renowned for its trendy renovated worker's cottages; cute cafes and shady, tree-lined streets. The house sat on a narrow block. A row of lush green agapanthus in full bloom lay on either side of a short path leading to the modern double doors she and Ben had spent hours choosing.

He kissed the side of her head. "Me too, my sweet. It's perfect."

Jayden, Ben's fourteen-year old son, raced past them with Bindy, his Scottish terrier, yapping at his heels. They headed directly for the backyard where Tessa's dog, Sparky, scratched at the gate and barked excitedly. Stephanie, Tessa's old house-mate, had dropped him off a little earlier. Tessa knew her energetic dog was excited to see her, but she wanted to inspect the inside of the house first. Grabbing Ben's hand, she pulled him along the path to the front door, letting out a small gasp as he whisked her off her feet and carried her over the threshold, kissing her tenderly as he placed her back on her feet.

He tucked a strand of hair behind her ear as he gazed into her eyes. "We should ask God to bless this home, before we do anything. What do you say?"

She smiled lovingly into his soft milk chocolate eyes. "That's a wonderful idea."

He kept his arm around her and she leaned her head against his chest as he thanked God for bringing them together and giving them a fresh start. "Father, your faithfulness and grace are amazing. Thank You for the gift of marriage and for all the good things You have in store for us. And thank You for this house. Please make it into a home where your love touches everything we do. We ask You to bless this home and this family. In Jesus' precious name, Amen."

"Amen." Tessa drew her head back and looked deep into her husband's eyes. She thanked God so much for bringing him into her life.

Persistent knocking on the expansive glass sliding door

leading out to the deck and pool area broke the moment. Jayden stood on the other side with both dogs at his heels, tails wagging and filling the air with short sharp yaps. Ben located the correct key and opened the door, letting Jayden in but holding the dogs back.

"Let them in, Ben." Tessa laughed as she picked Sparky up and cuddled him, trying to protect her face from his eager kisses. Bindy snuck in through the gap but Ben grabbed her before she got too far.

"They should stay out. They'll destroy our new furniture."

"Seriously?" Tessa arched an eyebrow. Although Steph had never been too happy about it, Sparky had been allowed inside their cottage whenever they were home, and she hadn't thought about him not being allowed inside here. Was this going to be their first disagreement? "Maybe we could just set some ground rules? They're smart—they'll learn, I'd hate them to be outside all the time."

She hugged Sparky to her chest as she waited for Ben's response. His gaze bounced between Tessa, Jayden and the two dogs.

"Yeah, Dad, the backyard's way too small. There's hardly any room for them to run around in. You've got to let them in."

Ben let out a slow sigh. "All right then. But they're not allowed on any of the furniture or upstairs. Agreed?"

Tessa winked at Jayden as they nodded their heads in agreement. His shy grin gave her hope that he might start to accept her, maybe not as his mother, but at least as a friend.

Reversing beepers sounded from the front of the house. Ben dashed to the door to meet the truck drivers, and she and

Jayden reluctantly put the two dogs outside for their own safety.

"I'm going to check out my room." Jayden picked up his box of bits and pieces and headed upstairs. "Hope it's bigger than the backyard…"

Tessa laughed lightly, but cringed at the sarcasm in his voice. Would he learn to be happy here? She took a few moments to pray for him and to look around her new home before Ben returned with one of the drivers and a load of boxes.

The next few hours were filled with unpacking boxes and finding new homes for all their belongings. Later, once the drivers had left and they'd eaten the dinner Tessa's mother had pre-cooked for them, they relaxed on their new soft leather sofa. Subtle lighting in the garden highlighted a range of lush tropical plants surrounding the pool, and Tessa could almost imagine she and Ben were still on their honeymoon.

"It's hard to believe we were in Fiji this time last night." She leaned back against his chest and gazed outside. "I wish we had longer before going back to work. This month has been wonderful. I don't want it to end."

"Me either, my sweet. We've got tonight and tomorrow, so let's make the most of it."

He nuzzled his face into her hair and sighed contentedly.

The next morning, Ben suggested they have breakfast out before tackling the remaining boxes. The rest of the day passed too quickly, but by the time evening came, everything was unpacked and in its place.

Tessa woke early on Monday morning to Ben kissing her forehead. “Good morning, sweetheart,” he said softly as he gazed into her eyes. “I’m going for my morning jog. Be back in twenty.” She returned his kiss and rolled over, warmth and contentedness enveloping her body as she curled up, cuddling his pillow. She was drifting off when a jolt stabbed her body and she sat with a start. *What am I doing? I can’t go back to sleep.* Her pulse quickened. She couldn’t be late for work, today of all days. The day she started her new job. She showered quickly and threw on a pair of pink scrubs. As soon as they were on, she realised they weren’t fitting for her new role as manager, and quickly changed into a white shirt and black trousers. She ran a brush through her hair, grabbed some pins off her dresser and finished putting her hair up as she ran downstairs to where Jayden was in the family room watching television.

“Good morning, Jayden,” she called out as she headed straight to the kitchen and turned the coffee machine on.

He glanced up and mumbled something unintelligible.

“Did you sleep okay in your new room?”

“Preferred my old bed.”

She inhaled slowly. *Be patient. Count to ten.*

“Do you always take so long to get ready?” He turned his head away from the television and looked at her directly.

She fought the temptation to tell him off for being rude. Instead, she replied in a controlled voice. “The new clinic’s right near here so I don’t need to get up so early. It’d be a different matter if I was still working at the old one.” She wasn’t going to tell him she’d slept in and was now in a rush.

“My school’s on the other side of the city. How am I getting there?”

"We've already talked about that." *He really is trying me out...* She clenched her fists and steadied her breathing. "Your dad will drive you today since it's your first day back after the break, but then you'll need to catch a bus most mornings."

She took a deep breath as he continued to glare at her. "You should be able to catch the same bus to the city as your dad, but then you'll need to change and catch the bus to Indooroopilly on your own. From there it's only a short walk to school." She held his gaze firmly as she paused. "Remember?"

"Dad used to drive me every day." His eyes narrowed.

"I know, but let's give this a try, shall we? It's not fair to expect your dad to drive through the city and then back to his work every day when you can catch a bus. It was different when you lived on the other side of town."

He shrugged and gave her a glassy stare before picking up his school bag and absentmindedly checking the contents. "Guess I have no choice, so I suppose we'll have to. Where's Dad?"

"Gone for his run. Should be back any minute." Tessa poured herself a coffee and sat at the breakfast bar, resting her elbows on the marble benchtop as she wrapped her hands around the mug and studied her new step-son. Her heart was heavy. *How am I going to get through to him, God? Please help me, I'm really struggling.*

She sighed as she sipped her coffee, letting the warm liquid slide down her throat, settling her. *He'd be a good-looking boy if only he'd cut his hair. But that doesn't matter, it's what's going on inside him that's important. He's been through so much, God, it's understandable he's struggling with everything. What child could ever understand why their mother would walk out on them without explanation? Even though he's surrounded by people who love him dearly, there must a deep ache in his soul.* Her heart cried for him. *I just want to love him and have him love me, Lord.*

But she had to earn that right. She couldn't expect a fourteen-year old boy who'd been through everything he'd been through to automatically accept her as his new mum.

"Jayden, I'm sorry if I was short with you. Let's try to get through this first week and then we can see if it's working. Okay?" Her voice was warm and much softer than before.

He stopped fiddling with his bag and looked up, tilting his head a little. His lips were still tight and he wore a pout on his face. "Whatever."

She cringed. She was starting to hate that word. "Tell me about all your sports and after school activities. I'd like to come and watch when I can—if you're happy for me to do that."

He leaned back and crossed his arms, studying her face as he reeled off his weekly schedule. "This term I've got rugby training on Mondays and Fridays, rowing on Tuesday mornings, and tennis on Wednesdays." He paused, as if waiting for her to say something, but then continued before she could. "I'm also part of the science club which meets on Thursday afternoons."

"Wow! All of that?"

His mouth lifted slightly at the edges, falling just short of a smile. "It's nothing." He shrugged again as if he were trying to play it down, but her reaction had obviously pleased him. "And you don't have to worry about watching me play. Dad hardly ever comes even though he says he will."

"That's not true. Your dad tries to get there as often as he can. You know he does." She couldn't help herself. He wasn't being fair on Ben at all. During their courtship, Ben was always having to hurry away to either watch him play something or other, or to pick him up. She'd occasionally gone with him, but most often she'd just let Ben go on his own. But that was about to change. She would go whenever she could. She stood her ground and looked him in the face. Jayden's smile had disappeared and his sullen look had returned, and it made her blood boil.

"Yeah, well, what you think is often and what I think is often must be two different things." He turned his attention back to his bag. "By the way, what's for breakfast?"

"Breakfast?" Tessa dropped her striped leather work bag onto the floor and slapped her forehead. "Breakfast! Of course, I nearly forgot." She let out a small laugh as she hurried into the kitchen.

Jayden sat with crossed arms watching her with amusement as she pulled out pots and pans and yanked food items out of the pantry.

"Stop looking at me like that! I'm not used to making breakfast for a family."

He flicked the television off and joined her in the kitchen. "We normally only have cereal and toast." He grabbed the packet of Weetbix from the cupboard and placed four of the breakfast biscuits into a bowl.

She sighed with relief and chuckled to herself as she leaned back against the counter. He'd been testing her again. Such a changeable boy. One minute he was horrid and the next he was joking with her. Was it typical teenage behaviour, or was it because he was working out how to treat her now she was his step-mum?

"Thank you." She gave him a grateful smile, and her heart warmed as a cheeky grin spread slowly across his face. Maybe, just maybe, they'd made some progress.

CHAPTER 2

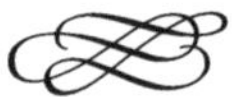

After Ben and Jayden left, Tessa spent a few minutes doing a quick tidy up before leaving for the Clinic. She reluctantly decided to take the car instead of her bicycle. Riding along the tree-lined streets, feeling the sun on her back and the breeze tickling her face always put her in a good frame of mind for work, but today she needed to make an impression. And she couldn't be late.

Pulling up in the parking lot of the New Farm Veterinary Clinic just before eight o'clock, Tessa sighed heavily when she saw several cars already there. She paused to settle herself before climbing out. The morning definitely hadn't gone to plan. Everything had been hurried, and the interaction with Jayden had left her drained. She and Ben had hardly said a word to each other. By the time he got back from his jog, he only had time for a quick shower and an even quicker breakfast. They had a very short Bible reading and prayer together, with Jayden sitting between them with crossed arms. Nothing like the leisurely breakfasts they'd had on their honeymoon and the extended devotions they'd enjoyed so much. They'd have to get up earlier in the future.

And now she had to face her new staff. Most of them she'd worked with at the old clinic, but there, she'd been one of them; now she was the boss. Why had she let Fran talk her into it? Fran knew how much she loved having hands-on contact with all the animal patients, but had insisted she'd make a great manager and convinced her to take the position. At least she had the option of reverting to her old job as head surgeon after six months if she didn't like it. *Six months!* Tessa sighed again. *Okay God, I prayed about this, and everyone seemed to think it was the right thing to do. I'm still not sure, so you'll have to be with me today. Please help me to manage my staff wisely. Thank you.*

She opened the car door and climbed out. The new clinic was impressive with its fresh paint job and brightly coloured murals of animals of all sorts covering the front and side walls. Fran had been busy. The old run-down building she'd bought for her second clinic was now warm and welcoming.

She glanced at her watch. Right on eight. No more time to procrastinate. She inhaled slowly and deeply before pushing the door open and entering her new work place.

THE STAFF MEMBERS were grouped around the reception desk and they all looked up as she entered. Two new faces. Fran had briefed her about Sandy and Harrison, but Tessa had yet to meet them. She greeted the group and introduced herself to the new members. Sandy Bowman had sharply arched eyebrows and a mole the size of a pen point above her top lip.

She talked with her hands and jiggled on the spot. "Today's my first day on the job," she told Tessa enthusiastically in a high-pitched voice.

"Is that so?" Tessa already knew this was the receptionist's first day of paid employment, ever. Fran had taken a liking to the young, enthusiastic New Zealander and was prepared to give her a go.

Sandy nodded, her face lighting up even further.

"You're not from around here, are you? Let me guess..." Tessa tilted her head and tapped her finger to her chin. "Across the Tasman Sea? New Zealand?"

A wide smile, showing a set of braced teeth, appeared on Sandy's face. "Yes! I grew up on a sheep farm, but we also had goats and pigs, and ducks and chickens. I've been around animals all my life."

Tessa laughed at Sandy's enthusiasm. "Fantastic. Glad to have you on our team."

She then turned her attention to Harrison Smith, the new surgeon. Lean and tanned with high cheekbones and big brown eyes, his black hair hung loosely around his shoulders. She was tempted to remind him to tie it back before he operated, but instead, she offered her hand. "Nice to meet you, Harrison."

He nodded and shook her outstretched hand, but his steady gaze unsettled her a little. As he leaned against the reception desk, he stuck his hands into the large pockets of his white lab coat and crossed one ankle over the other. *A little too cool for my liking.* But he'd come with excellent references, and Fran had raved about him.

Tessa excused herself and found her office just down the corridor on the left. Spacious and impressive, just like Fran's, a large, silky oak desk dominated the room. A row of matching shelves lined one wall, and a large occasional chair sat beside the window that looked out onto the busy main road. She hung her jacket on the coat rack behind the heavy door. From her work bag, she pulled out two framed photos and set them beside her computer screen on the desk. The first was of Jayden sitting on the beach beside Bindy and Sparky. The second was of her and Ben in front of the Tavoro Waterfalls in Fiji. She picked it up again and her pulse quickened as she gazed into her husband's loving eyes, and for a moment she was back there...

Sandy's high-pitched voice welcoming their first patient to the clinic interrupted her reminiscing. She replaced the photo and got to work.

By late morning, the vet clinic waiting room was full and Tessa's staff were stretched to the limit. The maximum wait time was meant to be twenty minutes, but some patients had been waiting for nearly thirty. She joined Sandy in apologising for the delay and offered refreshments to the waiting owners, something Fran would never do. She even handed out free treats to the animals.

Fran called around lunch time. Instead of the brusque, business-like tone she often adopted, Fran's voice was warm and congenial. "Hi, Tess. Just checking to see how everything's going on your first day."

Tessa flopped back in her chair. "It's way different to what I expected. We've been flat out all morning. I'm exhausted already. Did you send people our way?"

"No, but I've done a lot of advertising. Good to see it's paying off."

Tessa pressed a hand to her forehead. Outside her office door, Harrison shouted to his assistant to clean the surgical supplies. Working all morning without a break had made him demanding, and he seemed to resent Tessa dropping in to check on his work.

"I'm not used to managing staff." Tessa cupped her hand over the mouthpiece and spoke quietly. "I'm used to getting in there and doing the job myself, not standing back and letting them do all the work. I'm feeling a little frustrated."

"You'll get used to it. Your job is to manage, so as much as you're tempted to jump in and help, it's better if you don't, otherwise your staff will never take you seriously."

Tessa's sigh blew loose strands of hair from her face. That might be Fran's way of managing, but it wasn't hers.

"The first day is always the hardest. It'll get easier, and I've got faith in you. I wouldn't have encouraged you to take the job if I didn't believe you were the right person."

Tessa drew a deep breath. "Thanks Fran—I hope you're right."

"And remember, I'm just a phone call away, so don't hesitate to give me a ring if you need any help."

"Thanks, I'll remember that."

It was only the first day, but Tessa was already questioning whether she'd made the right decision.

CHAPTER 3

Tessa breathed a sigh of relief when the day finally ended and she was on her way home. She could hardly wait to change into more comfortable clothes and put her feet up for a few minutes before fixing dinner. She'd make sure Jayden didn't have to remind her about making meals again. Her first weekday dinner would be simple—chicken stir fry with noodles. Surely both boys would like that.

Arriving home shortly after her, Jayden dropped his backpack and a green and white training rugby ball onto the kitchen floor.

"Hey Jayden. How was school?" She looked up from where she was cutting vegetables. Her few moments of rest had been interrupted by a phone call from her mother.

"Fine."

A one-word answer. She had to think of a question that would require him to use more than one word. "Do you have any homework?"

"Already done."

Two words. Slightly better. "Dinner won't be ready for a while, so have a snack if you want."

His shook his head. "No, I'm fine." He sat down at the counter and picked up a pencil, twiddling it between his fingers.

"What's on your mind?"

He stopped twiddling. "I was going to wait and ask Dad, but I guess I can ask you." He raised his head and looked at her. "Can I stay over at Neil's house and go with him to rowing in the morning?"

Tessa stopped mid-slice. She bit her lip and frowned as she studied Jayden's face. Was this another test? *But more importantly, would Ben allow Jayden to go to Neil's house?* Maybe she should call him. She reached for the phone but then replaced it. She couldn't call Ben. He was in that important meeting this afternoon and wouldn't want to be interrupted.

"I've finished all my homework." Jayden pulled a notebook out of his backpack and showed her a page full of equations.

She put the knife down and perused the page.

"We've got some new music we want to work on, and after school is like the only time we can do it. And Neil's mum can drive us to rowing in the morning. It'll save Dad having to get up real early to take me."

Tessa tapped the counter with the tip of the knife. "Have you stayed over at Neil's on a school night before?"

"Yes. Dad lets me do it all the time."

Tessa studied his face. His eyes, normally sullen, gleamed, as if he were trying too hard to convince her. *Is he taking me for a ride? I wish I could call Ben and check.*

"Come on. It's okay. And you and Dad can have the night on your own."

A night on their own, how tempting was that? It had only been two nights since their honeymoon had ended, but it seemed like a year.

She blew out a slow breath. "I guess it's okay. As long as you're sure it's all right with your Dad."

"He'll be fine with it. Thanks." Jayden jumped up, looking like he wanted to hug her, but stopped himself just in time.

"One thing—can you drive me?"

Tessa burst out in laughter. The hide of the boy! She shook her head, but she'd do it to keep him happy and have the night alone with Ben.

"Come on then, let's go. Just make sure you're in time for rowing in the morning."

"I will," Jayden assured her. He ran upstairs and in a few minutes was back in the kitchen carrying a toothbrush, pyjama bottoms and his rowing clothes, all of which he stuffed into his backpack.

She drove him to Neil's, about a twenty minute drive away through busy afternoon traffic. He chatted all the way. Amazing how he could talk when he wanted. He was warming to her, and she was glad she'd decided to let him go.

He jumped out of the car and slung his pack over his shoulder. "Thanks Mum… I mean, Tess."

She started to say it was fine for him to call her Mum, but stopped herself. He'd do it in his own time, when he was ready. No use forcing it.

"Bye Jayden. See you tomorrow afternoon." She waved to him as he closed the door and headed up the driveway. She'd asked if she should speak to Neil's mum, but Jayden said it wasn't necessary. As she watched him disappear into the house, she hoped she'd made the right decision.

When she arrived back home, she finished the dinner preparation. She set the table, adding a couple of candles for a romantic touch since Jayden wouldn't be with them. Then she emptied her work bag and went to finish setting up her home office while waiting for Ben to arrive. Bindy and Sparky tussled one another and chased their favourite balls around the room before flopping down on a cushion under her feet.

Engrossed in stacking file folders and organising her books and papers, Tessa was shocked when she next checked the time —nearly an hour had passed and Ben should have been home.

She stepped into the kitchen and pulled a frozen coconut cream pie out of the freezer to thaw for dessert before picking up the phone to call him. As she was dialing, the front door opened, and Ben walked in.

"Ben!" She replaced the phone and ran to him, throwing her arms around his neck. "You had me worried. I was beginning to think something had happened to you!"

He lifted her up from the floor and kissed her forehead. "I'm so sorry, sweetheart, I didn't mean to be this late. The meeting ran overtime. I should have called you—I'm sorry."

"It's okay, I'm just glad you're home." She lowered her arms around his waist. She'd never tire of gazing into his eyes and feeling his arms around her. "Tell me—how did it go? Did you accept the partnership?"

He ran his hand through his hair and inhaled slowly. "No, I didn't. Even though they adjusted the terms in my favour, it didn't feel right. I feel like I've let them down. They've bent over backwards for me, but I wasn't convinced it was the right thing to do. For us." He brushed some hair gently off her forehead and ran his finger down her cheek. "I don't want to be tied down right now, even though it would have helped us financially."

"It must have been difficult. But it's over now, and you don't have to think about it anymore."

"Yes, it's a weight off my mind. And it means I can just do my hours and come home to my family. To you." He lowered his face closer to hers. Her pulse quickened… without Jayden at home, dinner could wait.

He pecked her lips and pulled away. She swallowed hard. She couldn't blame him. He didn't know they were alone. She'd have to tell him, but had she done the right thing allowing Jayden to go?

"Sorry Tess—later." Ben undid his tie and glanced upstairs. "Is Jayden in his room?"

The moment had arrived. She swallowed hard and let out a breath. Surely it wouldn't be a problem. Jayden had convinced her it was okay. But Jayden had been playing games with her lately. Hopefully this wasn't one of them, but she had that sinking feeling it was.

She tried to relax, but her body had stiffened. "He's at Neil's house. He said it'd be okay with you."

A shadow fell across Ben's face. "Neil's house?" His brows came together. "How could you let him do that?"

"He said you let him do it all the time."

"Come on, Tess, you know better than that. He hasn't been allowed to stay over since that incident with Owen and the drugs."

"He said Owen wouldn't be there."

Ben shook his head and his lips straightened into a thin line. "He's taken advantage of you, Tessa."

Her heart sank. She'd made a huge mistake. "I'm so sorry. He was so sincere, and I figured that since this move has been tough on him, it wouldn't hurt for him to be with his friend for one night."

"Neil's a good kid, but that brother of his is unpredictable, and Mary and Bill hardly have any control over him." Ben raked a hand through his hair. "He could come back at any time, and there's no telling what trouble he could get those boys into."

For a minute, Tessa thought Ben was going to put his jacket back on and go after Jayden right then. She couldn't handle this. They hadn't been married a month, and already she'd already made a mess of things. She reached for his arm. "I'm so sorry. I should have checked with you. It was thoughtless of me."

"Jayden's going to pay for this. It's not really your fault. He shouldn't have asked to go."

"Don't be too hard on him. He's just testing me out—I'll be warier in future."

She stepped closer and looked deep into Ben's eyes. "Are we okay?" She was pleading, but they had to be okay. She couldn't bear it if they weren't.

Ben met her gaze and his eyes softened. "Yes, we're okay." He ran a finger slowly down her hairline. "But I'll be having words with Jayden when he gets home tomorrow afternoon."

A pang of guilt stabbed her. If only she'd been more

thoughtful and less gullible, Jayden wouldn't be in trouble with his father.

"Let's eat." He squeezed her hand. "We'll deal with this tomorrow. In the meantime, I'll call Mary and check that Owen's not there."

Tessa lit the candles, but any romance had disappeared from the evening.

CHAPTER 4

When Jayden arrived home from school the following day, Tessa and Ben were waiting for him in the living room, having both finished work early. Tessa perched on the edge of the couch, nibbling her fingernails and eyeing Ben as he paced back and forth.

She'd tried her hardest to convince him to let it go this one time, but he was determined to have it out with Jayden. All night he'd brooded over it. She hadn't liked the way it dominated his thinking, and how easily agitated he'd become over this incident. This wasn't the Ben she knew. Stephanie had said that often you don't really know a person until you live with them, but Tessa hadn't believed her at the time. Maybe she was right. They hadn't even made love last night. The first time since they'd been married.

It would have been better if Ben had fetched Jayden straight away—at least the matter would have been dealt with then and there rather than allowing it to fester like a sore left unattended all night and all day. At one stage she thought he would, but in the end he decided to wait until Jayden got home from school.

All day at work, Ben and Jayden had been on Tessa's mind. She'd prayed constantly for them, asking God for his grace and mercy to abound in this situation. Jayden was in a fragile state, and she feared if Ben came on too hard, it might push him further away. But Ben was determined to make Jayden answer for his blatant disobedience. She felt sick to the stomach.

The front door opened. Jayden slid his backpack onto the floor and bent down to scratch Sparky behind the ears. He glanced up when Ben stood in front of him.

"Hey Dad, you're home early."

"Yes, you're right. How was school?" The crispness in Ben's voice made her shudder.

"Fine." Jayden was immediately on the defence. He looked up at his father's dark face before shooting a plea for help to her. If only she could have warned him before he faced his dad.

Jayden looked at his father again with narrowed eyes. "What's up?"

"Why did you tell Tessa that I allow you to stay at Neil's?"

Jayden's shoulders fell. "You used to."

"You know full well I don't allow it anymore. Ever since that incident with Owen." Ben's voice was tight, and he clenched and unclenched his fists as he glowered at Jayden.

"That happened a long time ago." Jayden's eyes darkened. "I learned my lesson. It's not like it's going to happen again."

"No, you're right. It's not going to happen again, because you're not allowed to be anywhere near Owen." Ben resumed pacing, every muscle in his body, rigid and tight. She'd never seen this side of him.

"What did you do last night?"

"We worked on our music."

"Was Owen there?"

"No."

"Are you telling the truth?"

"Yes."

Ben stopped pacing and stared at Jayden. Jayden turned his head away.

"You're not to stay there again. Do you hear me?" When he didn't answer, Ben walked closer and stood over him. "Look at me, Jayden. Stand up."

Jayden stood slowly, his face stony and his eyes full of hate.

"The way you took advantage of Tessa wasn't right. You knew you weren't allowed to stay at Neil's, and you shouldn't have told her you were. You're grounded for a month. Hopefully that will teach you to think twice before you act so foolishly again."

Jayden's shoulders slumped. "But Dad..."

Ben held his hand up. "No. That's the way it is. A month—you can go to school and to training, but no friends and no camp."

Jayden blinked in disbelief and then turned to Tessa, his eyes pleading with her. Without thinking, she rose and placed a hand on his shoulder.

"Ben, that's too harsh. Won't you rethink? He's so looking forward to camp." She hated the plaintive tone in her voice.

Ben drew his brows together and glowered at her.

She swallowed hard. This wasn't what she'd expected. Ben

was being way too tough on Jayden, and he'd never looked at her like that. Maybe she shouldn't have taken Jayden's side, but she had. Now she was caught between standing up for Jayden and supporting her husband.

Jayden pulled himself from under Tessa's hand, snatched up his backpack and stormed out of the room and up the stairs.

Tessa lifted her eyes slowly. Her lips trembled and a lump sat in the pit of her stomach. They hadn't had a single disagreement in almost a year of friendship and courting, and now they'd had two in a matter of days.

"Ben, I'm sorry." Her voice was shallow and she could barely speak. "I shouldn't have questioned you. It wasn't my place." Her heart pounded and tears pricked her eyes. She stepped closer and waited. The Ben she knew was kind and loving. He wouldn't let this come between them. She swallowed the lump in her throat.

Ben's face slowly softened. She met his gaze and held it before reaching out her hand and closing the gap between them. She lifted her hand and gently brushed it against his cheek. "I really am sorry." Tears welled in her eyes. She needed to feel his arms around her. To hear him say he loved her.

He placed his hand over hers and pressed it to his cheek. "I'm sorry too. I don't know what comes over me." His voice had lost its edge and he sounded genuinely distressed. "He riles me so much sometimes and I just can't help myself." He pulled her close and kissed the top of her head. She snuggled into him, squeezing her eyes shut to stop her tears from falling.

He pulled her tighter. "I shouldn't have gotten so angry. With him, or with you. I'm so sorry."

As she rested her head on his chest, the blanket of sadness slowly lifted from her heart.

"We'll sort this out. Tess. It'll be okay, you'll see." Ben's voice was soft and filled with remorse.

She nodded and wiped her eyes. Lifting her head, she looked deep into his eyes. "I just want Jayden to be happy."

"I know, but something had to be done. He did the wrong thing." Their eyes were locked as Ben brushed damp hair off her face.

She held Ben's gaze for a moment longer before leaning her head against his shoulder. Although she loved Ben with all her heart, it didn't change the fact that she didn't agree with him. Her heart was torn. She sighed heavily. She could do no more. Jayden was Ben's son, and she had no right to interfere. She'd have to trust his judgment, even if she didn't like it. She drew in a deep, slow breath and squeezed her eyes shut, forcing the tears lurking just below the surface away. *Oh God, please give me wisdom and strength. Help me love both Ben and Jayden. I don't want to go against either of them, you know that, but it seems I'm caught in the middle.*

She drew in a calming breath and pulled herself slowly away, once again meeting Ben's gaze. Her pulse quickened when he leaned down and kissed her slowly on the lips.

A short while later, he followed her into the kitchen, gently placing his hands on her shoulders as she stood in front of the counter. "Let me help." His deep voice and his lips on the curve of her neck sent a tingle through her body. She breathed in slowly. They would survive this.

She reached into the cupboard and pulled out three plates. Turning around, a slow smile formed on her face. "Okay, take these." Their eyes met. She leaned up and gave him another slow kiss before handing him the plates.

He took them and began to set the table.

She stood on the other side of the kitchen counter. As she checked the vegetables, her thoughts turned to Jayden upstairs. "Is he going to be all right, Ben?"

Ben paused, salt and pepper shakers in hand. "I hope so. I truly do." He sighed heavily and glanced upstairs before finishing the table.

"What else can I do to help?" He slid his arms around her waist from behind.

"Mash the potatoes."

"Where's the masher?" He nuzzled her neck, sending shivers of delight through her.

"In the drawer." She let out a small laugh as he let her go and fetched the masher. If only it were just the two of them, they would have such a wonderful time. But it wasn't. She'd known what she was taking on when she accepted his proposal, but she hadn't expected it to be quite like this. "Shall I see if Jayden wants to come down to dinner?"

Ben glanced upwards and nodded. "It might be best if you go instead of me." He gave her a grateful smile as he picked up the masher and attacked the potatoes.

TESSA HESITATED outside Jayden's room. Music, if you could call it that, blared through the door. She knocked once with no response. She knocked again, this time much louder. Still no response.

She opened the door a fraction. Jayden lay face down on his

bed, his body racked by the occasional sob. Her heart went out to him. She wanted to take him in her arms and hold him tight, but she hesitated. He probably would only push her away. If only she could make everything right.

"Dinner's ready, Jayden." Her voice was soft and caring. "Will you come down and join us?"

He turned his face to the wall. "I'm not hungry."

Tessa grimaced. Should she make him come down or wait it out? *God, what should I do?* Her parents would never have let her or Elliott dictate to them, even through their testing teenage years. But this wasn't the time to force the issue. For now, she'd let him be. It would only be her and Ben at the dinner table again tonight.

Ben looked up expectantly as she returned alone. She shook her head and knew the heaviness in her heart was written on her face.

As they ate their dinner, Jayden's empty chair and place setting highlighted his absence. Tessa prayed that Ben's tough stance wouldn't have a long-term negative effect on Jayden, but she feared it might.

When Ben finished eating, he placed his knife and fork neatly together on his plate and wiped his mouth with his napkin. "Thanks Tess, that was lovely."

"Thank you." She let out a small laugh. Ben was always so polite, but her cooking still left a lot to be desired.

Ben leaned back in the chair and folded his arms. "We haven't decided what church we're going to yet."

Tessa sighed. "Do we have to talk about that now?" They'd skirted the issue several times, and now with Jayden on her mind it was the last thing she wanted to think about. Besides,

Ben had indicated he wasn't keen on her church, and she wasn't keen on his, so they were at a stalemate.

"I think so. It's time we decided."

"Okay then, what are you thinking?" She resigned herself to hearing what she didn't want to hear.

"We have three choices. My church, your church, or we start afresh at a new one. I'm thinking we should start a new one."

A new one? She straightened. That could be the best option, although she'd miss Gracepointe. A change might also be good for Jayden. He hadn't been keen of late. And maybe it'd be fun starting a new church together.

"I think you're right. Do you have one in mind?"

Ben leaned forward and rested his elbows on the table, his eyes brightening. "I've done some checking—a guy from work used to go to the Fellowship Bible Church not far from here. He enjoyed it, and it's close by, so I think it's worth a try."

"Sounds good." She smiled warmly at him and squeezed his arm. She prayed that this might be the start of something good for them all.

CHAPTER 5

"Hurry up and get dressed, Jayden." Tessa carried the dirty Sunday morning breakfast dishes past him and headed into the kitchen. Jayden followed her sullenly. Ever since Ben had grounded him, he'd been even more moody and non-communicative towards them both.

"I *am* dressed."

She glanced at his ripped jeans and t-shirt and her nose wrinkled. He'd just finished feeding Bindy and Sparky, and the mud he'd picked up from the walk they'd taken earlier with the dogs had dried into dirty stains. Not a good look for making a first impression at a new church. "Why don't you put on something a little more presentable for church? The service starts at nine and we don't want to be late."

"I don't want to go to church." His mouth set in a hard line.

As she placed the dishes in the washer she counted to ten. Jayden was skilled at winding her up, but she was learning to think before she spoke, something that didn't come naturally.

At that moment, Ben walked down the stairs knotting his light blue tie. Had he heard what Jayden said? Would Jayden back down now his dad was here?

Ben glanced from her to Jayden. Her heart pounded.

"Have I missed something?" Ben slipped the knot in his tie up to his neck and adjusted his shirt collar. He looked so smart in his slim fitting dark trousers and tailored shirt. Tessa lifted her eyebrows and gave him an appreciative smile. In her simple summer shift and orange wedges, she felt a little underdressed. But that wasn't the issue at hand. Jayden's church attendance was of far greater importance.

Jayden didn't answer. Should she ignore what he'd told her, or tell Ben? Was this another of Jayden's tests? She'd certainly become warier ever since the Neil issue. She inhaled deeply and made her decision.

"Jayden doesn't want to come to church." She held her breath before glancing at Jayden. The filthy look he gave her said it all.

Ben turned sharply and faced him. "How many times have we gone through this? You're not old enough to make your own decision yet. You're coming, like it or not." Ben's voice was softer than in the past, but Jayden's eyes held daggers as he picked up a dog's lead and threw it on the floor. "Fine. But don't expect me to listen to any of that God stuff." He stormed off up the stairs.

Ben started to follow but Tessa grabbed his arm. "Let me go. Okay?"

He hesitated.

"Please Ben. You're too wound up." She rubbed his arm gently and prayed he'd calm down.

He released a slow breath and raked his hand through his hair. "You're right. You go. I'm not in the right frame of mind."

She reached up and kissed his cheek. "I won't be long." Letting go of his hand, she walked slowly up the stairs, her heart heavy. She paused in front of Jayden's door. *Lord God, please give me wisdom to know what to say. Let Jayden see Your love in me, and soften his heart, I pray.*

When she returned with a smile on her face several minutes later, Ben looked at her quizzically. "What did you say to him?"

"Don't be upset, but I told him if he goes to church every Sunday for a month, we'll take him and Neil away camping for a weekend." She put a hushing finger to Ben's lips as he started to object. "He agreed, so just be happy, Mr. Straight and Narrow." She flashed him a cheeky grin and stifled a laugh at the surprised look on his face. "Besides, a weekend away camping will be fun. How long has it been since you've been camping?"

Ben drew in a deep breath and averted his gaze. "Never."

"Never? Really? Well, it's about time you did."

He looked up. "I'm not sure I agree with bribing him to go to church." He had that serious look in his eyes again.

Her shoulders sagged. *He really is Mr. Straight and Narrow sometimes.* "I wouldn't call it a bribe. More a reward. And Jayden's coming to church happily. Isn't that worth it?"

Ben sighed heavily. "I'm not sure I like the way you went about it. It sounds like a bribe to me," he said in a serious tone. "I want Jayden to go to church and come to know God just as much as you do. I've been praying about it for years, but I'm not comfortable with this. I want him to go because he wants to, not because he's being bribed."

She took a step back. "So do I, but that's not going to happen right now in his frame of mind. Isn't it better that he comes willingly, for whatever reason? When I look at Jayden, I see a hurting kid, and I don't think you're doing much to change that by being so tough on him."

"Is that what you think, Tessa?"

She opened her mouth but nothing came out. They were arguing again, and just before church. Tears pricked her eyes and she willed them not to come out as she glanced away.

"We should have discussed this first before you offered him something we hadn't agreed on."

She cringed at his words. Jayden came down the stairs before she could respond. She'd completely stuffed up again. When would she learn? But Ben would never have agreed if they'd discussed it first. Why couldn't he see that what she'd done was okay?

"I'm ready." Jayden had changed into a pair of clean jeans and a plain button down shirt, but his cap was still firmly planted on his head. He looked at his dad and then at her.

She was determined not to let him see there was any problem between the two her and his dad.

"Hey Jayden, that's better. Let's go." She placed a hand on his shoulder and gave it a light squeeze. Ben would just have to be happy Jayden was coming to church. They'd deal with their problem later.

She tried making small talk on the short drive to church to cover the simmering tension between her and Ben. He was right—she should have discussed it with him first before suggesting something this important. But she couldn't ignore the fact that Jayden was sitting in the back of the car in a better mood.

Tessa reached out her hand and squeezed Ben's leg. He didn't respond. He just looked at the road ahead, his profile stiff and rigid. Her heart fell. *Oh, God, I don't want to go to church like this. Please help.*

CHAPTER 6

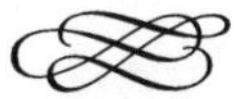

As they arrived at the carpark of the Fellowship Bible Church, Tessa was tempted to ask Ben to turn around and drive home. How could they enter a house of God when all was not right between them? Why wasn't he happy that Jayden had willingly come to church with them? Okay, she'd promised him a weekend away camping with Neil, but surely that was worth it. What was Ben's problem?

He climbed out, closed his door with more force than necessary, and strode around to open her door. Tessa inhaled deeply. She hated it when things weren't right between them. Could she do this? Walk into a new church, amongst people she didn't know, and pretend all was well? For Jayden's sake, she had to. Tears stung her eyes. She'd never in her wildest dreams imagined she and Ben would be at loggerheads over Jayden coming to church. Maybe her mum had been right and being a wife and mother to a teenager was harder than she ever thought it would be. But she had to pull herself together. She wiped her eyes, took a deep, slow breath, then fixed a smile on her face before taking Ben's hand and walking into the church that on the outside looked more like a warehouse than a place of worship.

At Gracepointe, old familiar hymns played on an organ welcomed everyone to worship. Here, a band belted out modern worship songs. What would Ben think? Being the ultra-conservative accountant that he was, surely he'd prefer the older, more conservative type of service they were both used to. Jayden, on the other hand, was more likely to feel comfortable with this type of music.

Although they were a little early, the main auditorium was almost full. People sang and clapped, and a warm sense of God's spirit filled the place. An older couple welcomed them at the door and directed them to some seats towards the back. Tessa glanced at Ben and squeezed his hand. Surely he'd let their disagreement go now they were in church. Her heart warmed when he returned her squeeze and placed his arm around her shoulder. She snuggled in close and thanked God for intervening, and prayed they would be able to resolve their differences. The lyrics to the song were on the screen, and as she sang, a spirit of renewal washed over her.

'Give me grace to see beyond this moment here

To believe that there is nothing left to fear

And that You alone are high above it all

You my God are greater still'

It was so good to be back in church. Although Fellowship Bible Church was larger than Gracepointe and definitely more contemporary, maybe, just maybe, they could make this place their spiritual home. Amid the excitement of her engagement to Ben, the romantic wedding and their subsequent honeymoon, she hadn't been to church for several weeks, and with everything that had happened already, it was good to be reminded of God's constant grace. Above all the problems at home and at the clinic, God was greater still.

Long after the time of corporate prayer was finished, she sat with bowed head. Her spirit had been moved by the worship and the prayer time, but she needed God to touch her deeper still, and so she poured her heart out to God. *Thank You for being here with me right now. I'm sorry for being so distant of late, and for trying to do things in my own strength. I knew being married wouldn't be a walk in the park, but I didn't think it would be this complicated. We've had one argument too many, and all over Jayden. Maybe Mum was right and I'm not ready to raise a teenager. Doing so... or trying to do so... is causing so many problems between Ben and me, and that's the last thing I want right now.* Tessa's heart was heavy, and she was so lost in prayer and busy sorting out her thoughts with God that she barely heard any of the sermon. Whatever the pastor said, however, must have touched Ben for he squeezed her hand several times. Looking up, she forced herself to focus on the last part of the sermon.

The pastor, a blond-haired, youthful-looking man in his early forties, was preaching on "Love in spite of..." He read from 1 Peter 4:8. Tessa knew the verse well. She said it quietly to herself, "Above all, love each other deeply, because love covers a multitude of sins."

"To love God and to love one another are the greatest

commandments given to us by God. If we believe that God is perfect and good and holy, which He is, then it's easy to love Him. But to love imperfect human beings with all their sins and foibles can be tough. It's natural to judge people for their weaknesses and faults, but if we follow the example of Christ, we'll find it easier to love others the way He loves us.

"How does Christ love us? He loves us in spite of ourselves. He loves us in spite of our sins, faults, failures, and stuff ups. He loves us unconditionally. This deep love gave Him the strength to die on the cross so that our multitude of sins could be covered, and that deep love still abides today. When we don't act the way God wants us to act, does He turn his back on us? No. When we say careless words, does He stop his ears to our prayers? I don't think so. He just goes right on loving us in spite of all that, and we must do the same to the people who are in our lives. We must love our bosses, employees or co-workers in spite of the fact they may be difficult to get along with. We must love our spouses in spite of the fact that they aren't perfect. We must love our children in spite of their occasional disobedience. God wants us to love one another deeply, in spite of..."

Tessa couldn't think of a timelier message. As they stood for the closing song, she prayed that God would help her love Ben and Jayden the way He loved her. With Ben's arm around her shoulder, peace settled in her heart, along with hope that all would be well with the three of them.

The pastor hurried to the back of the sanctuary when the service ended. He shook hands with each member of the congregation as they began to file out. He greeted Ben and Tessa with a broad smile. "I'm guessing you're new?"

Ben returned the pastor's smile and shook his hand. "Yes, we just moved to the area and this is our first time."

"Welcome, glad you decided to worship with us this morning. I'm Fraser Stanthorpe, by the way."

"I'm Ben and this is my wife, Tessa." Ben turned to her and placed his hand behind her back. "Our son, Jayden—" Ben looked to his other side, but Jayden wasn't there.

Tessa spotted him standing with a group of boys his age. "There he is. Looks like he's made some friends." She caught his eye and smiled, but he lowered his cap and turned away. What had she done wrong this time? She sighed and turned her attention back to Ben and Fraser. She had no idea how his mind worked.

"I thoroughly enjoyed your sermon," Ben was saying. "It was just what I needed to hear."

Fraser smiled. "I always pray God will use my feeble preaching skills to touch lives in some way, so I'm glad you appreciated it. Why don't you stay for a coffee and meet some of the members? My wife is around somewhere, probably fussing over the babies in the nursery." He laughed. "I'll try to find her and introduce you."

In the meantime, Ben and Tessa introduced themselves to some of the church members as they enjoyed the coffee and cakes on offer. Tessa was delighted to find that Sandy was a member there and they greeted each other—not as manager and clinic receptionist—but as sisters in Christ. As Tessa enjoyed the Christian fellowship of Sandy and the other women, she had a nagging feeling she was being watched. She turned around and scanned the crowd of laughing, chatting members.

She almost spilled her cup of coffee as she locked eyes with a familiar pair of steel-grey eyes. The sun-tanned face with unmistakable high cheekbones to which they belonged confirmed her suspicions. *Michael's sister, Sabrina.*

CHAPTER 7

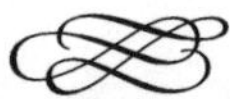

Tessa excused herself from the group of women she stood with and started toward Sabrina Urbane, but was stopped by Ben. "Jayden's already in the car. Are you ready to leave? The second service is about to start, so we should be going."

"Just a second." She shot a glance over his shoulder to where Sabrina had been standing a moment before, but she was gone.

Ben raised his eyebrows. "Looking for someone?"

"I thought I saw someone familiar, but never mind. Let's go." She bid goodbye to Sandy and the others before they left.

Ben took her hand as they walked through the church parking lot to their car. "I'm sorry for the way I reacted this morning and ignoring you on the ride over here. I didn't think before I spoke, but I know you love Jayden and want the best for him, and however you persuaded him to come, I'm glad he came with us today."

Was she hearing right? Ben was apologising? As much as she deplored crying at the drop of a hat, she couldn't help the glad tears that welled in the corners of her eyes. Her father had once told her that saying 'I'm sorry' is a sign of strength. She smiled gratefully at Ben now.

"I should have checked with you first before making any promises to Jayden, so I'm the one who should be the sorriest." She wiped her eyes with a tissue she already had in her hand. "But sometimes I do think you're too hard on him." She held her breath. Had she said too much again?

Ben stopped a few feet from the car and placed his hands on her shoulders, turning her to face him. "You might be right. I don't know." He rubbed her arms. "But never be afraid to be honest with me. Even if we don't see eye to eye on the best way to raise Jayden or other matters, let's try to agree to disagree. I can't stand the silent treatment any more than you can. And I'm sorry for letting my anger get the better of me. We'll get better together, I promise." He lifted her chin with his finger and kissed her lips. "And I guess I'll be happy to go camping."

The twinkle in his eye made her laugh.

THEY DECIDED to have lunch at Southbank, and caught the CityCat along the river from New Farm. Southbank buzzed with locals and visitors out enjoying the sultry summer's afternoon. Ben held her hand as they strolled along the promenade inspecting the various menus on display from the array of restaurants vying for their patronage. Tessa encouraged Jayden to walk beside them, but he hung back, much to her frustration. They chose an Italian restaurant and sat at a table under the shade of some large leafy trees. The breeze from the river occasionally reached them, as did the air conditioning from inside whenever a waiter came in or out. Tessa was glad she and Ben were back on speaking terms, and they enjoyed each other's company as they discussed the church service and made plans for the week ahead.

"I'd like to watch your rugby practice on Friday, Jayden. I finish work early, so I could come and watch and then bring you home. What do you think? Is that okay?"

He shrugged in an off-handed manner, as if he didn't care. "If you want."

She clenched her jaw and breathed slowly and deeply. She'd been trying everything to include him in the conversation, but he'd reverted to short retorts. Maybe it was typical of teenagers, but it was a hard slog.

"I think I can make it too. Tessa and I can both come and watch." Ben squeezed her hand.

Jayden lifted one shoulder and eyed his father. "Whatever."

What was wrong with the boy?

Ben jolted forward. Tessa grabbed his hand, holding him back. She breathed a sigh of relief when he eased back without pursuing Jayden any further.

She continued chatting with Ben, doing her best to include Jayden, but her efforts continued to be met with either a short answer, a half-hearted shrug, or a frosty stare. What had made him like this? He'd been happier and even a little chatty after she'd talked with him this morning and promised the camping trip. Church should have done him some good, but he seemed worse, if that was possible. She prayed for God to give her patience and understanding.

. . .

Back home a little later, Jayden asked if he could take the dogs to the off-leash park. Tessa was tempted to let him go alone, but instead, grabbed the opportunity to spend some time with him—she didn't care if he wanted her to come or not. Nothing was going to change if she didn't take whatever opportunities came her way, and Ben had already said he had some work to catch up on. Besides, she hadn't spent much time with Sparky over the past month, and a walk in the park with the dogs in the late afternoon sunshine appealed.

"Wait there. I'll come with you."

Jayden looked back with almost zero expression on his face as she grabbed her hat and hurried to join him. He threw Sparky's sky blue leash to her without turning his head when she stepped in beside him.

They settled into a leisurely pace as they walked along the shaded footpath. Most of the houses in the street were renovated workers' cottages, much like the one she had shared with Stephanie. They passed only one other new house. When they reached the corner, they had to side step the tables and chairs outside the local bakery which also doubled as a popular café.

The tantalising aroma of freshly baked bread and coffee wafted from the recently rejuvenated building. "We could have breakfast here next Saturday. It's nice and close, and the food looks great," Tessa said as she looked back at the freshly baked pastries on display in the glass cabinet.

Jayden didn't reply. Maybe teenage boys didn't like eating out with their parents, especially when they had no siblings to hang out with. As a teenager, she had Elliott to talk and joke with when they'd eaten out with their parents, and they'd all enjoyed their outings to Busseys. What would it be like to be an only child? Maybe Jayden felt he was an appendage, and that she and Ben would prefer him not to be there.

They reached the main road running down to the river and crossed to the other side where the park began. Huge Moreton Bay Figs created a cool avenue of dense shade leading to the river, and stems of blue and white flowers from lush green clumps of agapanthus nodded in the breeze. Tessa breathed in deeply and allowed the fragrance to tickle her senses. How easy it'd be to forget the task at hand. Jayden hadn't said more than one or two words since they'd left home. He'd said more to Bindy than he'd said to her. But that was why she'd come. She took a deep breath and tried again.

"How are you liking school so far this year, Jayden?" The question wouldn't elicit much of an answer, but she had to start somewhere.

"Fine." One word, but at least he didn't sound defensive. Exasperated, but not defensive. A slight improvement.

What did fourteen-year old boys talk about? Music? Girls? Pets? She'd have to give Elliott a ring sometime soon and get some suggestions from him. Sport? Maybe.... she inhaled and gave it a go.

"Out of all the sport teams you're in, which is your favourite?" She tried to make it light, not an interrogation, but would he see it that way?

He took a moment to reply. "Rowing," he finally said.

"Really? I thought it would've been rugby."

He shook his head. "It's fun to play, but I prefer rowing and tennis." The dogs stopped to sniff at a tree. Jayden toed the dirt with his shoe. "Dad played rugby when he was in school, and he was good at it. He won a lot of awards." He raised his head, meeting Tessa's gaze with the same milk chocolate eyes as Ben's. "He'd be disappointed if I didn't play."

Tessa's heart rose a little. Jayden was finally telling her something about himself. She wanted him to continue, but he looked like he'd already said too much and he lowered his eyes.

"Maybe you should talk to him about it. I don't think he'd mind if you dropped it."

"I never said I wanted to drop it," Jayden said sharply.

She'd got that wrong. They continued walking along the path heading towards the off-leash area.

Tessa took a deep breath and changed the subject. "If ever you want to talk about things, like how you feel about your Mum leaving, or about school or church, or anything, really, I hope you feel you can talk to me. I'm a good listener." She held her breath as she studied his reaction. He kept walking straight ahead, as if he hadn't even heard, but sniffed and wiped his eyes with the back of his hand.

"You miss her, don't you?" Her voice softened, and she struggled to hold her own tears back. How could Kathryn have done this to him?

He nodded as he wiped his eyes again.

Tessa placed her arm lightly across his shoulders. He didn't push her away, but he didn't look at her either. "You know, I think you're doing remarkably well given all that's happened. I can't even imagine how you must be feeling, but I'm sure your Mum still loves you."

He pushed her arm away. "Yeah—that's why she left me and

lives on the other side of the world. Funny way of showing love."

"She sent you cards and money for your birthday and Christmas, so she hasn't forgotten about you."

Jayden shrugged, but it was so obvious he cared and that Kathryn had hurt him more than she'd ever know.

Time to change subject again. "What kind of band are you and Neil planning?"

"One that makes music." Jayden's voice was full of sarcasm.

Obviously. Patience, Tessa. She drew in a breath. "I mean, what type of music do you play?"

"Heavy metal."

Her brows shot up. Ben wouldn't approve of that. "Do you have a name for yourselves yet?"

"No."

Back to one word answers. By the time they reached the off-leash dog park, Jayden had stopped talking completely and she'd given up asking questions. After watching him run and play with Bindy and Sparky for a while, she chatted with some of the other pet owners then took a stroll along the fence line. She gazed at the river where the shadows from the trees were slowly reaching across to the other side and shivered. Every time she started to connect with Jayden, he pulled away and it saddened her. Maybe he resented not having Ben to himself anymore. Or maybe he thought she'd walk out like his mum had. If that was the case, she'd have to find a way to reassure him she was in his life to stay.

The warmth was quickly disappearing out of the day, giving way to a cool evening. A jacket would have been sensible. As she watched Jayden run around with the dogs, her heart reached out to him. So much bitterness and hurt, and so young. "Lord God, please help me connect with Jayden. Help me love him like You do, and to see him through Your eyes, as a child of God, precious in every way. Pour Your love out on him and draw him to Yourself. Heal his hurting heart, Lord God. And please give me wisdom and patience in all I say and do, even when he ignores me or is rude to me. Thank You, Lord God for loving and caring for him. In Jesus' precious name, Amen."

CHAPTER 8

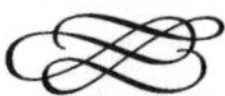

Ben glanced at the clock for the third time in less than five minutes and sighed, throwing his pen across the desk. It wasn't that important, anyway. The report could wait until tomorrow—no urgent need to do it tonight.

He should have gone with Tessa and Jayden. But maybe it'd do them good to spend time together. He picked up the photo of the three of them taken at the wedding. Jayden had really tried that day to be on his best behaviour. He looked so grown up in his dark coloured suit. He'd even had his hair trimmed and for once it looked tidy. *And Tessa*. Ben's heart skipped a beat as he gazed at his beautiful wife. All brides were beautiful, but she'd outdone them all. From the moment she'd appeared at the church entrance on her father's arm, he hadn't been able to take his eyes off her. Her face had beamed as she walked down the aisle, and her long flowing dress, her gleaming hair, her flowers, they'd all mesmerised him. How he loved her. But this past week had taken its toll. He hated it when they argued over Jayden. He sighed heavily and replaced the photo before closing his laptop computer and tidying his desk.

The house was quiet with nobody home. Normally, loud music blared from Jayden's room, or Tessa had the Christian radio station on. Quiet was nice. Peaceful. He strolled through the house, pausing in the living room. Tessa had thrown her bag on the couch beside her jacket. Why couldn't she put them away? Before they were married, he'd never noticed how untidy she was. How had he not noticed? He let out a small chuckle. Probably because he'd been so captivated by her stunning blue eyes and her fun, loving nature that nothing else mattered. But now they were living together, sharing their lives on a daily basis, little things about her annoyed him. But he wouldn't say anything—especially not today after their argument this morning. Instead, he picked her bag and jacket up and placed them in the bedroom where they belonged.

Their disagreement this morning still weighed heavily on his mind. Yes, they'd forgiven each other, but it shouldn't have happened. She was only trying to help, but she didn't know Jayden. Jayden would take advantage of her every way he could, and would have her wrapped around his little finger in no time at all if she pandered to him. The only way to handle him was by being firm.

Ben stood in the doorway looking out at the pool and deck area before stepping outside. Rays of light from the late afternoon sun shimmered through the trees and onto the pool. They'd barely swum in it, yet it was one of the reasons they'd chosen this house. Already life was too busy. He eased onto a wicker chair and tried to relax, but thoughts of Tessa and Jayden made him restless. He rubbed the back of his neck.

Maybe they could eat outside tonight. And maybe he could do something special. Try to make it up to them. His mind started to tick. He couldn't cook, so it was no use trying—it'd be a complete failure. But he could order pizza, and he could buy flowers for Tessa. And maybe he could suggest a game of chess with Jayden. That would surprise him. Jayden had never seen him play chess, but when he was younger, he'd often played with his parents, usually beating them, much to his father's displeasure.

Ben grabbed his car keys and headed out. Hopefully he'd have enough time to get everything before they got back.

TESSA AND JAYDEN strolled home in the last of the afternoon sunshine. Tessa didn't try to force any further conversation, instead, as she walked silently beside Jayden, she prayed for him. He turned his music up and listened to it through his earbuds. Very anti-social, but he was a teenager, so maybe it was the done thing. She tried not to take it personally.

As they neared the front door, something red caught her eye. *A rose?* She squinted to see it better. What would a rose be doing on her front door? Yes, a single red rose with a small card attached had been wedged into the door frame. She carefully pulled both from the door, and, holding the perfectly formed rosebud to her nose, inhaled the beautiful perfume. She opened the card and her hand flew to her chest as she read, *'A beautiful rose for my beautiful Tess. I love you with all my heart. Ben xxx'*

"Oh Ben." Tessa lifted the rosebud to her nose again before

opening the door and peering in. He was nowhere to be seen, but the tantalizing aroma of freshly cooked pizza floated through the house. Jayden had taken the dogs around the back, and outside on the deck, he and Ben were leaning down and patting the dogs, *and talking.* She paused and gazed with love at her husband. So handsome, and so caring. He said he had work to do, but instead he'd gone out and bought flowers and pizza. The outdoor table was already set. Two pillar candles flickering in over-sized glass holders, a wedding gift from Stephanie, shed soft light onto the table. The solar garden lights highlighting the greenery around the pool and the gentle trickle from the water feature reminded her of their bure in Fiji, and her heart overflowed with love for her husband.

He rose slowly as she stepped outside onto the decking. She met his gaze. Her pulse quickened as she walked slowly into his arms. He lowered his lips and kissed her gently, leaving her in no doubt of his love.

"I thought you were working..."

"Shh..." He put his finger to her lips. "Let's just enjoy this moment."

"But what about Jayden?"

"Don't worry your beautiful head, Mrs. Williams. Jayden's getting the pizza ready. We're safe for a few minutes." He took her in a loose dance hold as soft music played in the background. She moved in time with him, swaying to the rhythm of the music, and thought she was in heaven.

"We need to do this more often," she whispered into his ear.

"Yes, we do." His deep voice sent tingles down her spine. When he spoke to her like that, it was easy to forget all the arguments they'd had, and she fell in love with him all over again. He kissed her slowly, and for a moment, she forgot all about Jayden.

She reluctantly pulled away when Jayden appeared beside them carrying a tray of piping hot pizza. Ben left one arm around her waist as he turned to face Jayden.

The poor boy. She and Ben had tried to keep their physical displays of affection private as much as possible, but Ben had set this up, so he must have decided it was okay this time. Nevertheless, Jayden's face had reddened, and she couldn't help but feel for him.

"The pizza smells wonderful, Jayden. Let's eat while it's hot." She moved away from Ben and placed her arm lightly on Jayden's shoulders as they moved to the table. The aroma of melted mozzarella, salami, and Italian herbs made her stomach rumble.

"This is a perfect way to end the weekend. Thank you." She smiled lovingly at Ben as she reached her hand out and found his under the table.

"It is, I entirely agree." Ben's eyes lit up as he squeezed her hand and returned her smile. He took a slow breath before tearing his gaze away from her. "Let's give thanks before we eat."

Tessa grimaced when Jayden rolled his eyes, and as Ben gave thanks for the meal, for the day, and for his family, she prayed silently for him.

Later, she was surprised when Ben brought out a chess set. "I didn't know you played chess. How many more secrets have you got?" she asked with a touch of mockery in her voice.

"Ah, not many, my love. But you'll have to wait to find out."

She hit him playfully with the back of her hand, but as their eyes met, her stomach fluttered. How she'd love to wrap her arms around him and tell him how sorry she was for questioning him and how much she loved him, but he had a chess match to play. Instead, she curled up on the outdoor lounge and pretended to read while he and Jayden played chess. Her heart warmed as she watched them interacting so easily. All was going to be well in the Williams' household.

CHAPTER 9

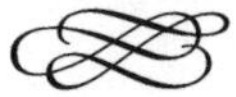

Three weeks later, Tessa locked her sky blue Hatchback and headed to the cinema entrance. After yet another argument with Ben that morning, she'd considered cancelling her lunch and movie date with Stephanie, but in the end, had decided to go. A few hours with her best friend would probably do her the world of good, and maybe put some perspective into everything. Not that she wanted to bare all to Stephanie, but if the opportunity arose, maybe she could share a little.

She scanned the area to see if Stephanie had already arrived. She wasn't half obvious. Standing at the ticket booth, dressed in casual brown balloon pants and white crepe top, her long auburn hair popped with red highlights. She whirled around when Tessa called out.

"Tess! Great to see you!" She gave Tessa a massive hug, almost pulling her off her feet before drawing back and holding her at arm's length. "You're looking fantastic. Married life must be suiting you."

You didn't see how long it took to cover up my red eyes. Tessa determined to put on a brave face and not let Stephanie see how upset she was. Though the argument with Ben gnawed at her deep down, and sat like a heavy lump in her stomach. How could they be arguing like this again? She drew a deep breath and planted a smile on her face.

"You're looking pretty good yourself, Steph. Love your hair!"

"Had it done this week. You really like it?" Stephanie ran her hand through her long locks, holding it out so the red highlights gleamed.

"Yes, it really suits you."

Stephanie linked her arm through Tessa's and they strolled inside, talking non-stop as they headed for one of the cafés they used to frequent when they were housemates. Tessa tried to focus on what Stephanie was saying, but she couldn't shake the horrible words she'd shouted at Ben just before she left. They rang in her ears and in her heart, making her feel sick to her stomach. How could she have told Ben he was the hardest, coldest person she knew? *God, please forgive me, I didn't mean what I said. You know that.*

Standing at the front of the café, she could barely think about what to order. Her appetite had fled, and in fact, the very thought of food turned her stomach. She had to get something, so she ordered a grilled chicken burger. Stephanie ordered a vegetarian pizza. They decided on a table towards the back where it was quiet.

"Seems ages since we caught up. My fault, I'm sorry." Tessa

forced herself to converse normally, all the while pushing back the tears that loitered just below the surface.

"Perfectly understandable. You're newly married, so that's the way it should be."

"Yes, I guess so." *But I miss relaxing together without any pressure.* Tessa picked up her glass of apple cider and wrapped her hands around it. When they were on their honeymoon, she and Ben had relaxed together all the time. What had happened to cause so much friction? She could easily break down there and then and tell Stephanie exactly how she was feeling, but she wouldn't. She'd pull herself together and focus on her friend. She straightened and lifted her chin. "How's your new housemate going?"

"Don't start me..." Stephanie rolled her eyes. "Hannah makes you look tidy. She never puts anything away, I have to wipe the bathroom vanity after her every time, and the kitchen's always a mess."

Exactly what Ben says about me... Tessa exhaled sharply. "Give the girl some rope. She's only young, and she's never lived away from home before."

"And don't I know it." Stephanie humphed, blowing some straggly hair off her face. "Anyway, enough of Hannah and my woes. Tell me all about you. How's your job? How's Ben?" As Stephanie sat forward, steepling her hands, Tessa felt she was under a microscope.

She gripped her glass. If she held it any tighter it would break. *Here we go...how do I get out of this?* She took a deep breath. *Start with the job...*

Stephanie waited expectantly for a reply.

I shouldn't have come... Tessa swallowed the lump in her

throat and took hold of herself. *Just talk normally. Forget you've had an argument with your husband and don't know where he is.* She drew another slow breath and lifted her chin. Stephanie peered straight at her. Tessa forced herself to answer. "I'm not sure I'm cut out to be in management. Fran says she's happy with my work, but I miss the hands-on contact. I only get to do surgery when we're really busy or when Harrison's away. And that's my passion—always has been. I'm a vet, not a manager." Her shoulders slumped. Why had she let Fran talk her into taking it on?

Stephanie reached out and squeezed her wrist. "It's early days yet. Give it some time. At least Fran gave you the option of returning to your old job if this one doesn't work out."

"I have a feeling I'll be taking her up on it as soon as the six months are up."

Tessa glanced up as the waitress delivered their meals and scurried off to the next table.

"And Ben? How is he?" Stephanie placed her napkin on her lap and cracked some pepper over her pizza.

"He's good." Tessa tried as hard as she could to make her voice sound normal, but it caught in her throat.

"Tessa—what's wrong?" Stephanie leaned forward and searched her face.

Tessa pushed back the tears welling in her eyes. She was not going to break down in front of Stephanie. She was going to pull herself together and be strong.

"Nothing. Nothing's wrong." She took another sip of her cider to gain some time and to avoid Stephanie's prying gaze.

Stephanie raised her eyebrows, but her voice was soft. "I've been your friend for years, and I know when something's bothering you, so don't say nothing's wrong. If you don't want to tell me, that's fine, but if you need a sympathetic ear, well, here I am."

Tessa let out a resigned sigh. A sympathetic ear would be good. *Oh, why not? It might even help.* She let out a wobbly laugh as she grabbed a tissue from her purse and blew her nose. "You know me too well." She clenched her hands together in her lap and gazed into Stephanie's caring eyes. "This might surprise you, but I'm beginning to think Ben and I argue too much, and we haven't been married that long." Her voice caught again. Verbalising her concerns made it all the more real, and it hurt deep down. She didn't want to argue with Ben. She loved him. How could they be arguing this much?

"Hmmm." Stephanie leaned forward, resting her elbows on the table. "Ben doesn't strike me as the arguing type."

"I didn't think he was either, but he's so fussy about everything. I thought you were bad enough, but he's something else." Tessa pinched her lips tightly together and leaned closer. "Yesterday afternoon I did all our washing and he commented on how I folded his socks, and then he actually rearranged the entire drawer. The entire drawer!" She threw her hands in the air. "I mean, they're just socks!"

"Calm down! Lots of couples argue over sock drawers." Stephanie's eyes sparkled with amusement and she let out a small chuckle.

"You're not taking me seriously." Tessa folded her arms and pouted. She shouldn't have said anything.

"It's pretty normal. I once counselled a husband and wife who couldn't stop fighting over what shows to watch and they'd been married for over fifteen years. They finally decided to get rid of their television set."

Tessa raised a brow.

"True story. But to be honest, I'd be more concerned about you and Ben if you didn't have any disagreements at all. It's absolutely normal as long as you manage it right and don't go to bed angry or upset. And I bet the making up bit is worth it." Stephanie's face expanded into a playful grin.

Tessa's eyes widened and her head jerked up. "Stephanie Trejo! Nice girls don't talk about things like that!"

"Sorry! It's just what I've heard." She flashed another cheeky grin before growing serious again. Reaching out, she gently placed her hand on Tessa's arm. "But something more than a sock drawer is troubling you. I can see it in your eyes."

How does she do it? Tears stung Tessa's eyes and she turned her head away. "I don't want to talk about it." She sniffed and wiped her eyes.

Stephanie moved closer and placed her arm gently over her shoulders.

Tessa closed her eyes, and inhaling deeply, swallowed the lump in her throat.

"You're right. There is something more." She lifted her head. "It's Jayden. Ben and I disagree on just about everything regarding him—his friends, his church attendance, school events, even what he wears." She wiped her nose and turned to face Stephanie. "Jayden isn't the easiest kid, but Ben's so strict with him. He keeps telling me I'm too soft, but what else can I do? Most times Jayden doesn't even want to talk to me." She sighed dejectedly. "I often don't know who to side with—Ben or Jayden." And that was the truth of it. She really was in a no-win situation. "I don't think I should have to side with either of them—we're supposed to be a family. We should be together, but we're not." The pain in her chest deepened as fresh tears stung her eyes.

Stephanie squeezed her shoulder. "You *are* a family. I know you want to be the best wife and mother, but maybe you're trying too hard. You and Ben are two different people and you're still getting used to each other. And Jayden has to get used to having a female in the house again. *And* he's a teenager… we all know what they're like." Stephanie let out a small chuckle.

Tessa sniffed as she rolled her eyes and nodded. *Yes, I know what they're like.*

"And he's still getting over having his mum walk out. It's a big change for you all, and as with most changes, it takes time to accept and adjust to a new situation." Stephanie brushed Tessa's damp hair off her face and tucked it behind her ear. "It might take six months or a year for you all to understand each other and to work together, but you'll get there. I know you will." She smiled warmly into Tessa's eyes. "The main thing is to try not to change each other. Ask God to help you accept each other as you are, even the things you don't like. It'd be a boring world if we were all the same. But remember, Jayden is Ben's son, and despite how you feel, you need to respect Ben's decisions regarding him."

Tessa let out a frustrated sigh and slumped in her seat, crossing her arms. "What if I don't agree with him?"

"That's something you need to talk about together. And pray about. You're both sensible adults, and you both love Jayden, so that's not the problem, but somehow you're going to have to find a way through this. But Tess," Stephanie squeezed her hand and looked her in the eye. "Ben is Jayden's dad, and you need to allow him to take the lead, even if you don't agree all the time. But talk with him—don't argue. And don't worry too much about the small stuff. Work out what's really important and just learn to let the rest go, as usually it doesn't matter. You'll work it out, I know you will."

What Stephanie was saying was right, but it was oh, so hard. It would take time, but she and Ben loved each other. That was the main thing. Everything else, including their problems with Jayden, would get sorted, eventually. Tessa breathed in slowly, her heart a little lighter and feeling slightly more hopeful. "Deep down I know all that, but in the heat of the moment I forget it, and I say things I shouldn't and then regret it. Like today." The horrible words she'd spat at Ben flashed through her mind, bringing a fresh wave of tears to her eyes. She'd have to go home and apologise. And soon.

"You know you can always talk to me. I'm only a phone call away."

"Yes, I know." She sniffed and gave Stephanie the warmest smile she could muster. "It was silly not calling you earlier. It's been building for a while and I stupidly let everything start to get me down. And then we had this argument this morning…"

"I only know about marriage in theory. But I know it can be the most challenging, and the most rewarding of relationships, but it takes work, especially when there's a step-child involved." Stephanie opened her blue, nylon tote backpack and took out three paperbacks. "Here." She passed them over. "I ordered these books a while ago not knowing you were having problems already. Seems God might have had a hand in it." Her eyes twinkled.

"This is very kind of you. Thank you." Tessa smiled warmly at her friend as she took the books and inspected them. Christian books on step-parenting—just what she needed.

"My pleasure. I hope they'll help, even in a small way. Now, let's go watch our movie."

CHAPTER 10

Several hours later Tessa drove into the carport and breathed a sigh of relief. Ben's car was parked in its normal spot. *At least he's home.* She turned off the engine and sat. All through the movie she'd struggled to keep her mind on what was happening on the big screen, although she'd been wanting to see the latest Meryl Streep movie for some time. All she could think about was her argument with Ben that morning and what she'd say to him when she got home.

It had started the night before at the dinner table when Jayden had pleaded with Ben to allow him to go to camp, but Ben hadn't been prepared to discuss it. "No. You're grounded, and that's that." Ben wore a determined expression on his face. "You can't go to camp, and I don't want to hear another word about it."

Jayden glowered at him before he pushed back his chair and fled up the stairs to his room. The door slammed. Tessa's heart fell. She knew how desperately Jayden wanted to go to camp. All his friends were going, and he'd told her he thought his dad was being totally unfair. She hadn't told him she agreed with him, but she did harbour similar thoughts.

Ben rose and started to follow him. She grabbed his hand and pulled him back. "Won't you let him go?" She was pleading, but she didn't care. He paused. Their eyes locked. She held her breath and waited.

His expression didn't change. He shook his head. "No. I can't go back on what I said. He has to accept that it's part of his punishment."

She bit her bottom lip while she held Ben's gaze. Why couldn't he give in just this once? Her heart ached for Jayden. If only Ben could go a little easier on him, she was sure Jayden would be a much happier boy. But Ben seemed determined to see the punishment through, whatever the cost. She inhaled deeply and held her tongue. "Let him calm down for a while, then."

Ben let out a slow breath and she felt the tension in his body ease. He ran his hand through his hair. "You're right. I'll talk to him later."

While Ben was taking a shower, Tessa took the stairs two at a time and knocked lightly on Jayden's door. "Jayden, can I come in?" He didn't reply, so she knocked again, a little louder.

The door opened and she tentatively poked her head in. Jayden had flopped back on his bed. His sullen expression hadn't changed, but the hurt in his eyes tugged at her heart.

"Hey."

He didn't reply. He picked at the strings of his guitar and lowered his gaze.

"I just wanted to see if you're okay." Her voice was soft, caring.

He shrugged. "I hate Dad," he said, almost under his breath.

His words tugged at her heartstrings. She stepped into the room, weaving her way between dirty clothes and towels and perched on the edge of the bed. "Jayden, look at me." She waited. After three long seconds, he slowly lifted his eyes. "I'm sure you don't mean that. You're just angry with him, that's all. Your dad's only doing what he thinks is right because he loves you. He's not doing it out of spite or for any other reason."

Jayden's eyes watered. She inched closer and placed her arm gently around his shoulders. "There'll be other camps. And your month of being grounded is almost up."

"But I want to go to this camp." He shrugged her away and folded his arms. His lips trembled and he was close to tears.

"Oh Jayden, I don't know what to say, except that your dad's not going to change his mind, so somehow you're going to have to accept it."

He sniffed loudly. "I'm not going to talk to him ever again."

She let out a slow breath. *God, I don't know what to say to him. Please help him accept this.* "I think your dad's coming to see you soon, so you might need to."

He pressed his lips together before sinking lower into his pillows and turning to face the wall.

Maybe sleep would be the best thing for him.

For the remainder of the evening she and Ben avoided the topic, but it simmered away under the surface, placing an invisible strain between them.

. . .

THE FOLLOWING MORNING, before Jayden was up, Tessa sat beside Ben at the breakfast table. He read the Bible passage for the day, Colossians 3:12, "Therefore, as God's chosen people, holy and dearly loved, clothe yourselves with compassion, kindness, humility, gentleness, and patience." She knew the verse well, but wondered how Ben could read it and not be showing any compassion and kindness towards Jayden.

When he closed his Bible, she knew she had to say something. Surely he could see how hypocritical he was being. She placed her hand on top of his and looked deep into his eyes. "How can you read that verse and not show compassion to Jayden? He so much wants to go to camp, and it's just putting a bigger wedge between the two of you. Can't you let him go? Please?"

Ben drew a slow breath and held her gaze. The determination she'd seen the night before in his eyes had eased, and instead he wore a softer look, offering hope that he might change his mind. He squeezed her hand, but as she waited, his expression altered. "It's not a matter of showing compassion or not. Regardless of how much he wants to go to camp, I can't go back on what I said. It's a matter of discipline. He has to learn." Ben leaned forward in his seat, crossing his arms on the table. "I feel sorry for him, but that's the way it is. I'm sorry if you don't agree."

She counted to ten. Her heart pounded. Ben was so rigid towards Jayden. Couldn't he show just a little leniency? She could understand Ben not wanting to back down, but couldn't he see he was pushing Jayden further away? She inhaled slowly, but adrenalin pumped through her veins, and her body tensed.

And then she said it: *"Ben, you are the hardest, coldest person I know, and I doubt you care for Jayden at all."*

She pushed her chair back and fled up the stairs, just like Jayden had done the night before and she hadn't spoken to Ben since.

Now outside the house, her heart pounded. She'd been just as guilty as Ben but in a different way. Where was her kindness, humility and gentleness this morning? How could she have said those words to him? She had to apologise,

Apart from her relationship with God, her relationship with Ben was the one of most importance. Yes, she loved Jayden and felt his pain, but it would do Jayden no good to see her and Ben fighting. Especially over him. But could she really put aside her own beliefs on what was right or wrong, let go of her need to make things easier for Jayden, and trust God to work everything out for good as he promised in the Bible?

She rested her arms on the steering wheel and bowed her head. *God, I'm sorry for the horrible words I spoke to Ben this morning. Please forgive me, and please give me the words to assure Ben that I truly do love and respect him, and that I'm sorry for the way I keep questioning his handling of Jayden. I so desperately want to be the wife that Ben wants and needs, and I feel so bad that we're constantly fighting. Please be with me now as I go and face him, and help us to work this out. And be with Jayden. Soften his heart, oh Lord. Thank You for your everlasting, unconditional love. Amen.*

She opened the door and slid out. Taking a deep breath to steady herself, she walked along the pathway and entered the house. All was quiet. *Jayden must be out.* She placed her purse and jacket on the couch without thinking, but then picked them up and carried them to the bedroom, hung her jacket in the closet and deposited her purse on the dresser.

She felt, rather than saw, Ben entering the room behind her. Her heart raced. What was he thinking? Those horrible words she'd said to him rang in her ears. How could she have said them? To Ben of all people? The kindest, most considerate person she knew. Just not with Jayden. Her hands shook as she slowly turned around.

His eyes were dark with pain, his jawline set rigid. She searched his face and swallowed hard. She stepped toward him, arms extended. "Ben..." Her voice wobbled. "We need to talk."

He stood still, his eyes fixed on hers.

She gulped as she reached out and took his hand. "I didn't mean what I said this morning. I said it without thinking, and it's not what I believe. You're a man who stands by his word, and if you said that Jayden was grounded for a month, and that included camp, it would have gone against your principles if you'd given in and let him go. I can see that now."

She stepped a little closer. "It was also wrong of me to lose my temper and yell at you. Jayden should never hear us argue." She searched his eyes. The darkness was receding, but he remained silent. What was he thinking?

"I never knew it was going to be like this." She took a deep breath and swallowed hard. "I guess I had this idealistic view that once we were married everything would be okay, and that the three of us would all get on together." Tears pricked her eyes. "I never dreamed I'd be put in the position of choosing which of you to side with. But Ben..." A sob caught in her throat as she closed the gap between them. "I know it'll be hard sometimes, but from now on I'll try my best to support you in front of Jayden and not to argue so much." She squeezed his hand. "I can't promise to agree with you on everything, and I'd love it if we could discuss how to handle him and try to come up with a compromise when we disagree." She gazed into his eyes. "I love you more than anything, and I'm truly sorry for what I said." Her heart raced as she waited for his response.

Their eyes remained locked. After several long seconds, he reached out his hand and brushed a finger along her brow. "We're both at fault. I know I'm hard on Jayden sometimes, but I do really love him, you know that." His deep voice was soft and caring. "And I love you with all my heart." His adam's apple bobbed in his throat as he swallowed. "I'm sorry I get grumpy." He placed his hands lightly on her shoulders and looked deeply into her eyes. "I don't want to be like that with you. Or with Jayden." He lifted her chin. "We'll get better at this. I love you deeply, and I'm sorry."

Her heart filled with relief and love as he lowered his face and kissed her gently.

"Let's ask God to show us the way through this," he whispered into her ear as he placed another kiss on her cheek.

A tear slipped from her eye as she nodded.

He wiped the tear away with his thumb, and took her hand as they knelt together beside their bed. He led in prayer, his deep voice full of conviction and humility. "Dear Heavenly Father, thank You for bringing Tessa into my life. You know how much I love her." His voice caught in his throat. "I'm so sorry for the times I appear uncaring and cold. Oh Lord, please help me be more compassionate and understanding, and to love Tessa the way You do." He paused and took a deep breath.

"Forgive my hardness of heart, Lord. Please soften me, and do with me as you will."

She squeezed his hand as his voice choked again. When he continued, his voice was quiet and subdued. "And God, please show me how to reach Jayden. I've failed him so often. Let him know how much I love him, and how special he is to me."

Tessa placed her arm around Ben's trembling shoulder and drew in a slow breath, very aware of God's presence with them. Her spirit, moved by Ben's brokenness before God, was heavy with conviction and a real desire for God to touch and to heal. "Oh Lord, bless our family. Bless Ben. Such a wonderful, strong, compassionate man who loves You so much. Draw us closer together, dear God, and help us be more loving and kind with each other when things get tough. Help us love each other, despite everything. And help us to show your love to Jayden. We look forward to the time when he sees for himself how wide and deep Your love for him is and he accepts Jesus as his own personal Saviour. Thank You, Lord God, for times like these when we're drawn to our knees, totally aware of our dependence on You. I'm Yours, dear Lord, let me live each day with Your love shining through me, especially to Ben and Jayden. In Jesus' precious name, Amen."

Tessa wiped a tear from her eye as she and Ben remained silent in God's presence, resting in His peace and allowing Him to reach deep into their hearts. She began humming one of her favourite worship songs, *"Be still and know that I am God; Be still and know that I am God; Be still and know that I am God."* Ben joined in, and together they worshipped, allowing God to renew their hearts and minds.

A short while later, Ben helped her to her feet and pulled her close. "Never doubt my love for you, Tessa."

"Nor you mine." She lifted her face and gazed deep into his eyes. He traced her hairline with the tips of his fingers. When he lowered his face to kiss her again, Stephanie's words ran through her mind. Making up almost made the argument worthwhile. Her heart rate increased, but then the front door slammed. *Jayden!* Tessa's pulse raced. She reluctantly pushed Ben away and patted her hair down. How could they have forgotten about Jayden?

"That was close," Ben whispered with a glint in his eye. He kissed her quickly on the cheek. "To be continued." His eyes flashed with mischief as he stepped into the bathroom and washed his face.

Tessa straightened her slightly crumpled shirt, checked her face in the mirror, and ran downstairs ahead of Ben. Jayden sat in the family room, Bindy and Sparky collapsed at his feet. Sweat dripped from his red face, and his skin glistened.

"Jayden, get off the couch—you're dripping all over it! You know what your dad will say." He looked up at her with hardened eyes. Her heart fell. The peace and confidence she'd felt only moments earlier had fled. Nothing had changed outwardly. Jayden was still angry with them both. But she and Ben were together, and God was with them.

"It's okay." Ben's deep voice reverberated down the staircase. Tessa's head jerked around as he came down the stairs and her eyes widened. Had she heard correctly? Ben said it was okay for Jayden to stay on the couch, sweaty and wet? She met his gaze—his softened eyes melted her heart and the smile she sent his way was filled with love and appreciation.

Jayden also looked up, an incredulous stare on his face.

"How was your run? Looks like you wore the dogs out." Ben bent down and patted first Sparky and then Bindy. Their heads lifted slightly, but their tongues continued to loll, leaving drool on the tiled floor.

"It was good." Jayden's voice was tentative, as if he didn't know how to respond to his father's out of character behaviour.

"I'm sorry for being so tough on you." Ben sat on the couch beside him. "Maybe I've been too tough, I'm not sure." He ran his hand over his head. "It was only because I love you, and I believed it was for your own good, but maybe I could have been more lenient." Jayden raised his eyebrows. "I can't go back on what I said, so no, you can't go to the science camp."

Jayden's eyes darkened again and he pursed his lips.

Tessa stood, unable to move, unable to breathe. *Dear God, please give Ben the right words to say, and please soften Jayden's heart.*

"But… if I'm right, tomorrow is the fourth Sunday, and so if you come with us to church again happily, I guess we need to decide where and when we're going to go camping."

Jayden looked up, his whole face slowly expanding into a wide grin.

"Really? You're going to come camping?"

Ben drew in a breath and then let it out slowly. "Yes. Not sure what I'm letting myself in for, but yes, I'll go camping."

Warmth spread through Tessa's body as her eyes blurred with tears. *Thank You, thank You God.* Catching Ben's gaze, she beamed at him with all the love in her heart.

CHAPTER 11

The following day, neither Ben nor Tessa had to rouse Jayden—he was ready before either of them. He still sat in church with a bored look on his face, but Tessa prayed that God would keep knocking on the door of his heart, and that one day Jayden would let him in.

At lunch, sitting outside on their deck, she asked him where he'd like to go for their camping trip. He'd been quiet after church, but he wasn't being rude or sullen, and she was heartened.

"Would you prefer the beach or the mountains?" She passed him the bowl of potato salad.

He took a few moments to reply. "I think I'd like to go to the mountains so we can go hiking and have a camp fire, and sleep in little tents, just like I did in scouts."

She'd never seen him so animated. "Just what I was thinking." She smiled at him, pleased at his enthusiasm.

Ben's face paled. Tessa giggled and squeezed his shoulder. "Come on Ben— it'll be fine!"

He shook his head and inhaled deeply. "Can't we rent an apartment on the Gold Coast instead?" The pained expression on his face made her feel sorry for him, but she couldn't help laughing.

Jayden rolled his eyes. "Come on Dad, it'll be fun."

While she and Jayden continued to make their plans, Ben remained quiet. They agreed to go on the Easter weekend in a month's time, leaving on the Saturday morning, and they'd head up into the hinterland behind the Gold Coast. Tessa knew lots of great camping and hiking spots, and she was sure her parents would lend them some camping gear.

OVER THE FOLLOWING WEEKS, she and Ben became more involved in the activities of the Fellowship Bible Church. Ben joined a men's prayer group that met twice a month, and she joined a weekly women's Bible study group that met on a Tuesday evening. Jayden continued going to church on Sundays, but didn't join any youth activities, and she eventually stopped pressing him about it. *God, it's up to You now. I can't push him any more. I trust You to bring him to Yourself when he's ready.* She prayed for him daily. Her heart went out to him—a boy in turmoil, confused and hurt. If ever she came face to face with Kathryn, she'd have words to say, that was for sure.

The first time Tessa went to the Bible Study she was a few minutes late, and all heads were bowed in prayer when she arrived. She quietly slipped into an empty chair beside an older woman with greying hair.

She settled into her seat, but instead of closing her eyes, she glanced around the group of perhaps twenty-five women. Her heart skipped a beat when she recognised the woman on the far side of the circle. *Sabrina Urbane.* Tessa hadn't seen Sabrina since that first Sunday when they'd locked eyes, and she hadn't really given her a second thought, assuming she must have just been visiting, but now it seemed she and Sabrina were to meet again.

For whatever reason, Sabrina had never been friendly with her, but after her decision to break up with Michael, the tension between the two of them intensified. Sabrina blamed her for Michael's depression and suicidal tendencies, and now, the last words Sabrina had spat at her nearly two years ago came ringing back: "If you truly love him," she'd said, "you would have stayed with him."

As the prayer session ended, Tessa slunk down in her chair and pulled her hair over her face in an attempt to become invisible to Yvonne, the group leader whom she'd chatted with briefly at church. *And to Sabrina.* It didn't work. Yvonne smiled at her broadly and welcomed her to the group. As Tessa thanked her, Sabrina stared at her with steely grey eyes.

Tessa lowered her head to avoid making any further eye contact with Sabrina. *Lord, why does she have to be here, at this church, in this group?* She opened her Bible to the passage in Esther the group was studying, but struggled to keep her mind on the discussion.

Could Sabrina have had a change of heart? Unlikely, given the stony look on her face. Seeing Sabrina made her think about Michael. It wasn't any of her business now she was married, but part of her wanted to know how he was doing. *Was he angry at her like Sabrina? Was he still on drugs? Is he still alive?* A twinge of guilt nibbled her conscience. They'd been so close for so long, and yet she hadn't even cast him a thought since meeting Ben. Did she dare ask Sabrina about him after the group meeting was over? She lifted her eyes but lowered them quickly as she met Sabrina's cold stare. *Not a good idea.*

"Okay, ladies, that's it for this evening. Let's close in prayer," Yvonne said at the conclusion of the study, closing her Bible and setting aside her notes.

Instead of joining in with the group prayer, Tessa closed her eyes and asked God to give her wisdom should she and Sabrina speak. And to forgive her for allowing her mind to wander when she should have been concentrating on the Word.

After the prayer time finished, the older woman sitting beside her introduced herself. "I'm Margaret Smith. Good to have you here with us. Are you new to the area?" Margaret reminded Tessa of Rose, Pastor Stanek's wife, with her greying hair, warm smile and overall cheerful demeanour.

"Not really, I've lived in the area for some years, but I've recently married, and my husband and I have just moved into a house together and started coming to this church."

"Well, I hope you enjoyed tonight, and that you decide to come back." Margaret patted her hand. "Come and let me introduce you to some of the others." Tessa forced a smile. *Not to Sabrina, please...*

As Tessa spoke to several of the other women who also welcomed her warmly, she searched the room, hoping her lack of attention wasn't being noticed. Sabrina wasn't there. Making a spur of the moment decision, she excused herself and hurried out. Sabrina was in the parking area, unlocking the door to her blue Porsche.

Clenching her fists, Tessa steeled herself. *Lord, I'm not sure why I'm doing this, but please be with me.* She called out to Sabrina. "I didn't know you lived in New Farm." Tessa bit her lip as she stopped in front of her. *What a stupid thing to say.*

Sabrina didn't look up. Instead, she opened her car door and tossed her purse inside before turning around. She flicked her long dark hair over her shoulder. Her black jeans fitted a little too snuggly, and her white button-up shirt accentuated the roll of fat bulging over the waist band and her more than ample chest. Her cold grey eyes bored into Tessa's. "What do you want, Tessa?"

Tessa hesitated a moment. What *did* she want? Did she really want to find out about Michael? Wouldn't that be opening a can of worms? But yes, if she were honest, she *did* want to know. She'd loved him, after all. And she still cared. She took a deep breath. "Just wondering how Michael is."

"You'd know if you hadn't left him." Sabrina arched her brows and planted her hand on her hip.

Tessa gritted her teeth and sighed. "There's no need to keep acting this way. It isn't right for you to keep blaming me for Michael's problems. I did everything I could to help him, but he wasn't prepared to take any responsibility for his actions or do anything to help himself. In the end I had no choice. You know that."

"Really? Do I?" Sabrina pursed her lips. "You ran away when he needed you the most instead of standing by him and helping him. You left him to struggle on his own." Sabrina stepped closer, pointing her finger at Tessa. Tessa drew back to get away from her, but Sabrina moved with her.

"You're a runner, Tessa Scott Williams. Whenever things get hard, you run away from them instead of working through them. And you're also stuck up, selfish, and you care for no one but yourself." Her nostrils flared as she held Tessa's gaze for a moment before climbing into her car and slamming the door behind her.

"How dare you—" Tessa blurted hotly but the engine of Sabrina's Porsche rumbled to a start, drowning her words.

"He's still in rehab, if you're interested," Sabrina called out the window as she sped off, sending a spray of gravel into the air as she accelerated.

Tessa breathed heavily as she stared at the car disappearing into the distance. Her hands shook and her head pounded. How dare Sabrina yell at her like that and call her those names! She had a mind to tell Ben they should find another church.

All the way home, Sabrina's words played over and over in her mind, but by the time she reached home, she'd calmed down somewhat and was already having second thoughts. Was Sabrina right? Had she done the wrong thing by leaving Michael? *Was she really a runner?* Could she have helped him more if she'd tried harder and stayed longer?

Parked in the darkened carport, Tessa rested her elbow on the car door, placing her head in her hand as she blinked back tears. *"God, I love Ben, You know that. I believe You brought us together and mean for us to be together forever, but there's no denying I used to love Michael and I do care about what's happened to him."* She gulped as a pang of guilt hit her. *"I'm not sure what to do. If I did do something wrong, I'd like to make it right, somehow. Lord, please guide me."* She straightened. *"But God, about Sabrina—I have no idea how to pray for her. Such a rude, spiteful person. I don't know how she calls herself a Christian."* Tessa drew in a deep breath. *"I'll have to pray for her another time, I'm sorry, God."* She climbed out of the car and took a steadying breath before entering the house.

CHAPTER 12

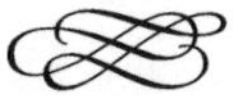

Late the following afternoon as Tessa was in her study completing some supply forms for the vet clinic, Jayden knocked on her half-opened home office door.

"Is it okay if I run Bindy and Sparky down to the park?"

She turned around and smiled at him. It was so good to see him happy. "Yes, that's fine, but don't stay out long. I heard thunder a while ago and it could rain. I don't want you to get caught in it."

The phone ringing in the kitchen drowned out her last words. She rose to get it, but Jayden waved for her not to bother. "I'll answer it."

Tessa nodded her appreciation. She could do without the distraction. She turned her attention back to the forms but snatches of Jayden's low voice floated into her office. She couldn't distinctly hear what he was saying, but he was on the phone for a long time. Tessa assumed it must be one of his friends. Sometime later, the back door slid open and Jayden left with the dogs.

Ping! Tessa's computer gave a short, high-pitched ding. A new email. She ignored it for a while, but eventually it got the better of her. She clicked on her email account. Not one, but three new emails. The first message was from Harrison asking if she'd talked with Fran yet about the pay raises she'd mentioned she was considering since the clinic was much busier than expected and the staff were run off their feet. She chewed on her lip. No, she hadn't done that yet but needed to. She'd meant to consult with Fran about it earlier in the week, but it had slipped her mind. She made a note to herself to call Fran first thing in the morning to discuss the matter.

The second email message was from Margaret Smith welcoming her to the women's Bible study group at Fellowship Bible Church. *'It's been quite a while since we've had a new member, and I'd love to get to know you better. If you're free on Saturday, would you join me for lunch at my place? All my children are grown and have left the nest, and my husband will be away for the weekend, so I'd appreciate the company. Let me know!'*

Tessa quickly typed back a response saying she didn't have anything planned and would be glad to join her for lunch.

Tessa's eyes widened at the last email message. It was from Michael. She read the name twice to make sure she hadn't made a mistake. Her heart pounded as she hovered over the message. Should she open it? How did he know her email address? She looked again. He'd sent it to her old address. Had Sabrina told him about their Bible study run in? Too coincidental if she hadn't. Tessa considered ignoring it or even deleting it, but as she hovered over the delete button, at the last minute she clicked to open it. It was only an email after all.

'HELLO TESSA,

It's been a while since we talked, a real long while, but when Sabrina told me you were asking about me, I had to contact you. I felt sure you'd have forgotten all about me, so I was glad to hear you hadn't. I've missed you, Tessa, more than words can express. Last time we were together I was a mess and I treated you badly, but I've cleaned my life up and sorted my problems. I finally did what you said and got help and have been in a rehab centre here in Sydney for the past six months. I should have done it much earlier, then maybe you wouldn't have left me. What a stupid person I was. Whatever the case, I feel the best I've felt since the accident.

The people here at the centre are fantastic. Most of them are Christians, and a few weeks ago I started attending chapel services and asked Jesus back into my heart. I'm so happy, Tess, and am filled with such peace.

There are so many things I want to talk with you about, and I'd really like to see you again. I guess you've moved on, and after all I put you through, I don't expect you to readily invite me back into your life, but I'm hoping we could put the past behind us and at least try being friends again. I'll be checking out of rehab in two weeks and I plan on staying with Sabrina for a week or so. Maybe we can meet then. Looking forward to seeing you.

Yours,

Michael'

. . .

TESSA SAT in front of the computer, re-reading the message several times. Her pulse was racing but she wasn't aware of it. It was too much to take in. Michael was better, and he'd recommitted his life to Jesus—the two things she'd prayed so long and hard for after he'd become hooked on those drugs. Such wonderful news she could hardly believe it. *Thank You God. Thank You so much.* Tessa sighed contentedly and leaned back in her chair.

It would be wonderful to see him again, to clear the air between them. After all the years they'd been together, to have it end like it did had left a heaviness in her heart. They'd been the perfect couple. He was the college sports hero, the boy every girl wanted to date, but she was the one who'd caught his attention, and he chose her, Tessa Scott, to be his girl. And they'd been inseparable for years.

Even when she continued at University after he dropped out, "I need a break from studying," he'd said after doing just one year, they'd still made it work. He'd massage her feet while she struggled with assignments, and he'd surprise her with impromptu outings and romantic gifts. One night when she'd been sitting at home with Stephanie, cramming for an exam, he'd dropped by and put a blindfold on her and whisked her away in his car. She'd protested. "I need to study, Michael," she'd said as he led her out, but she giggled the whole way until he took the blindfold off and she found herself at the top of Mt Coot-tha, looking out at the twinkling lights of the city below. He'd packed a midnight feast, and Tessa laughed with him as they devoured chocolate and ice-cream and drank cold pop.

But then he had that accident…

Tessa bolted upright in her seat. Something about his email

wasn't right. She read it again. Then it dawned on her. She sucked in a breath and her hand flew to her chest. *Sabrina hasn't told him I'm married!*

That would be right. Sabrina loved stirring things up. *But why wouldn't she have told him?* Would Michael be hoping they could be more than friends? *Probably.* She would have to set him straight. Tell him she was married and that it was too late. They could never be more than friends. Hopefully that news wouldn't cause a relapse.

She was just about to type a reply when she heard the key turn in the front door. She clicked out of the message and closed the lid of the computer before stepping into the hallway. Ben stood in the entrance, soaked from head to foot. His short brown hair bristled with water, and droplets fell from his nose.

"Ben—you're drenched!" Tessa grabbed a towel from the hall closet and handed it to him.

He dried his hair and face and peeled off his wet clothes, leaving a puddle of water on the floor. "I should have taken an umbrella to work. It started just after I got off the bus and I had to make a dash for it." He sounded breathless as he balanced on one foot and took a sodden sock off the other.

"You should have called, I would have picked you up. Here, pass me your wet clothes."

She took all his wet things and headed towards the laundry.

"Where's Jayden?"

Tessa hit her head with her hand. How could she have forgotten about him? He and the dogs were out in this. Michael's email had made her forget everything else.

"Tess?" Ben stood on one foot drying the other.

"He went to the park. I'll go find him." She threw Ben's wet clothes into the tub and grabbed her keys before heading out the door, but just as she was unlocking the car, Jayden turned up, soaking wet and out of breath, carrying Sparky.

"Sorry. I would've been back earlier, but Sparky got into a fight at the dog park."

"A fight?" Her heart pounded. "Is he all right? I hope he didn't start it."

"No, it was the other dog. And I think he's okay. He's just got some blood dripping from his ear."

"Let me look." Jayden placed Sparky on the ground and she bent over him. Blood wasn't just dripping from his ear, it oozed. He whimpered as she inspected the damage.

"You're a lucky boy, Sparky, it's just a small tear. But you shouldn't have got yourself into a fight." She gently picked him up and carried him to the outdoor wash tub. Jayden followed with Bindy close behind.

As she was applying ointment and a butterfly clip to the injured ear, Tessa remembered the phone call Jayden had taken before leaving. "Who was it who called earlier? You seemed to be having a good chat."

He froze momentarily before shrugging. "Just some lady. She had the wrong number but wanted to talk for some reason."

"That's odd." Tessa drew her eyebrows together and studied his face. Was he hiding something?

SHORTLY AFTER, once Ben, Jayden and the dogs were dried and clean and all the puddles had been wiped off the floor, Tessa turned her attention to dinner. Ben offered to help.

"I bought a cooked chicken at the supermarket on my way home, so we're just having that and some chips and salad. Maybe you could cut the chicken?" Tessa placed the chicken in front of Ben on a cutting board.

"Sure, no problem." While he dissected the chicken, she prepared the salad, but her mind wasn't on lettuce and tomatoes. She couldn't shrug off the message sitting on her computer.

"Is something the matter? You seem a little distracted. You haven't been having job troubles again, have you?" Ben looked up from the chicken and leaned against the kitchen bench.

She continued cutting vegetables. "No, everything's fine. I just have to catch up on some order forms tonight." *Should I tell him about the email?*

"Something's bothering you. I can tell." He put down his knife and stepped behind her, placing his hands lightly on her shoulders and gently massaged them.

She gulped. Why was it so hard to tell him about Michael's email? Was it because deep down she knew he wouldn't be happy about Michael wanting to see her? But *why* should he be unhappy? She had nothing to hide. She'd told him all about her relationship with Michael, and he'd been fine with it, so why was she now feeling anxious?

"Tess?" Ben stopped massaging and stepped closer. The familiar fragrance of his cologne tickled her senses. *Surely he'll be okay with it. I should tell him.*

"Yes, there is something." She continued slicing the tomatoes, but her hands trembled. Ben's breath was warm on her neck. She inhaled slowly. "Michael contacted me today." She continued working on the vegetables but held her breath as she waited for Ben's response. He didn't say anything but his hands tensed on her shoulders.

She reached for the salad dressing. "He's apparently sorted himself out and has recommitted his life to Christ." She was talking too fast. "He'll be here in Brisbane in a couple of weeks' time."

Silence filled the air. She wasn't game to move. Why was Michael contacting her turning into such a big problem?

"What's that got to do with us?" Ben's voice was controlled and steady, but she could tell he wasn't happy.

She turned around slowly and fixed her eyes on his. "He wants to see me."

Ben's eyes darkened. "Does he know you're married?"

"I don't think so." Her voice trembled. "He's been in rehab for the past six months."

For a long moment they stood, eyes locked. Her heart pounded. She didn't like the way Ben was looking at her, as if he didn't trust her.

"I don't see there's any need for that."

Her breathing quickened and she clenched her jaw. What was his problem? *There's only one man I love, and that's Ben. I just want to see Michael.* She shouldn't have told him. "But I'd like to," she said quietly.

Ben dropped his arms from her shoulders and moved away. He stood in front of the floor to ceiling windows and crossed his arms as he stared out into the grey drizzle.

She stepped closer to him. "I'd just like to see Michael to clear the air between us. Nothing more."

Ben shook his head as he whipped around. There was a glimmer of raw pain in his eyes but then his expression hardened. "I don't understand why you would see the need for that, Tessa. The past is the past, and that's where it should stay. I'd rather you didn't see him."

The sharpness in his voice shocked her. She'd never expected Ben to be so adamant. She felt like standing up to him, but thought better of it.

"Okay, I'll think about it. Don't worry about it for now." She moved closer and placed her hands on his chest. It was no use keeping the argument going. She looked up into his eyes and smiled. "There's only one man I love, and it's you." She stretched up and kissed him on the lips.

LATER THAT EVENING when she returned to her study, Tessa quickly finished the order forms and turned her attention back to Michael's email. She was tempted to reply and tell him how much she'd look forward to meeting up with him, but something stopped her. However incensed she was about having Ben dictate to her about whom she could or could not see, she hesitated to blatantly go against his wishes.

She leaned back in her chair and allowed her mind to drift. What would it have been like if she'd married Michael instead of Ben? Doubtless they would have had more fun. Michael definitely knew how to have fun. But would he have been a good husband? She rolled her chair towards the bookcase and rummaged through the box on the bottom shelf. She finally found what she'd been looking for—the photo of her and Michael taken at Moreton Island on his birthday. She blew the dust off the glass and held it up. His grey eyes and tanned, chiselled face stared out at her. Although she had no right to feel this way, she couldn't help the small pang of regret that ran through her body as she gazed into his familiar face.

She drew the photo closer. What would he look like now? Would the drugs have altered his good looks? But more importantly, how had he changed now he'd recommitted his life to God?

The more she thought about him, the more she wanted to see him. Not to rekindle anything—just to say she was sorry for deserting him like she had, because despite Sabrina's rude manner, what she'd said had hit a nerve, and Tessa had begun to think that she was indeed a runner.

She replaced the photo and reread his email. She should reply, but what would she say? Could she tell him she was married in an email? But if she didn't… Just then, footsteps sounded in the hallway and she quickly closed the lid of her computer.

CHAPTER 13

A few days later, Tessa was bringing in a basket of clean laundry and had to jump out of Jayden's way as he raced for the phone. She stared after him as he skidded to a halt and picked it up.

"Hello," he answered eagerly, but after hearing who it was, his expression changed and he handed her the phone. "It's Stephanie."

Tessa took the phone from him and placed it between her ear and shoulder as she carried the basket into the bedroom. "Steph, how are you?"

"Not good." Stephanie's voice caught in her throat.

Tessa plonked the basket onto the bed and sat beside it. "What's wrong? You're not crying, are you?"

"I have been." Stephanie sniffed. "You're not going to believe this, but I was fired this morning."

"Fired? What for?" Tessa straightened.

"When I arrived this morning, Rod walked into my office

and told me my services weren't needed anymore." Tessa heard fresh sobs collect in her throat; her friend was barely able to get the words out.

"That's terrible. What reason did he give?"

"Seems I'm not cut out for the job. All my case studies have been subpar and none of my recommendations seem to improve situations for the long term." Stephanie drew in a shaky breath and blew her nose.

"Don't say that. You're good at helping people sort their problems, like you did with Ben. In fact, you're the best counsellor I know."

"You mustn't know many, then." Stephanie succumbed to a fresh wave of sobs.

"Is there something you're not telling me?" A sinking feeling had developed in Tessa's stomach as the probable reason for Stephanie's dismissal occurred to her.

Stephanie continued to sob quietly.

"C'mon, Steph, what happened?"

Stephanie blew her nose again before answering. "Rod said it was because of breach of client confidentially."

I knew it. Tessa held her tongue.

Stephanie sucked in a deep breath. "When we lived together, I used to tell you about my patients. You warned me not to. I should have listened." She went quiet for a moment. "You told me I'd get in trouble for it."

"I'm so sorry. Can't they give you another chance?"

"I've already tried. I promised Rod I'd never do it again, but he wouldn't budge. I just don't understand how he found out. I mean, you're the only one I talked to about my clients and you'd never tell anyone." Stephanie gasped. "Ben! He's the only other one who knows."

"No!" Tessa's breath caught. "Ben would never do something like that. He loves you like a sister."

"He wasn't pleased when he found out I'd told you his life story. I wouldn't put it past him."

"You're overreacting. You're upset. But don't blame Ben. I have no idea how Rod found out, but it wasn't me, and it wasn't Ben."

"Well I don't know who, then." She began to cry.

"Stephanie, listen to me. You're good at what you do, and you'll get through this." Tessa paused. What advice could she give to someone who normally was the advice giver? *God? What can I possibly say that will help?* She breathed in slowly as words formulated in her mind. "What would you say to me if I came to you and told you I'd lost my job?" She waited. Stephanie took her time, but when she finally answered, her voice was steadier.

"I'd tell you that God was in control and you needed to trust Him."

"Yes, and..."

Stephanie sighed, and Tessa imagined her rolling her eyes. "God can work all things for good for those who love Him and are called according to His purposes."

"And..."

"Tessa! Stop it!"

"No, I won't. You know the theory—now it's time for you to put it into practice. And you can't go blaming others for your own mistakes—you know that. I'm sorry I'm being so blunt, but it needed to be said. How many times did I ask you not to disclose confidential information to me?"

Stephanie sighed heavily. "I know. It was wrong, but how can I tell my mum? She'll be so disappointed." She succumbed to a fresh wave of sobs, making Tessa wish she could be beside her to comfort her. But Ben would be home any minute and she hadn't got dinner ready. Maybe Stephanie could come to them.

"Come over for dinner. It won't be anything fancy, but we can talk more about it then. And we can pray.

"I can't face Ben. Not yet. I'm sorry, Tess. But thanks." Her voice caught again, and she swallowed hard.

Tessa exhaled slowly. She was torn. Should she drop everything and go to her friend, or stay here for her husband? Her grip tightened on the receiver. *God, what should I do?*

She made her mind up. "I understand, but Ben won't bite your head off. He truly does care for you. I'll try to pop over a little later, but hang in there, okay? By the way, is Hannah there?"

"No." Stephanie struggled to get the one word answer out. "But she should be home soon."

"Okay good. I'll call you after dinner and let you know if I can make it."

"Thanks." Stephanie sobbed into the phone.

"I'll pray for you in the meantime. But listen to me. It's not the end of the world. God can teach you a lot of things through this if you're willing to learn." Tessa closed her eyes and wrapped her hands around the receiver. She hadn't meant to sound quite so harsh. Stephanie's sobbing on the other end of the phone tugged at her heart. "I'm sorry. I didn't mean it to come out quite like that."

"It's okay. I deserve it."

When the phone clicked, Tessa sent up a quick prayer for her friend. She felt bad about the way the conversation had ended, and hoped Stephanie would be all right.

WHEN TESSA TOLD Ben the news about Stephanie's dismissal, he wasn't surprised. "You can't get away with doing the wrong thing forever. Eventually you get caught."

"But she assured me I was the only one she'd spoken to about her patients, so I don't understand how Rod found out."

"I had nothing to do with it, if that's what you're intimating."

"I know you didn't." She hesitated, and reached out her hand.

He narrowed his eyes. "But Stephanie thinks I did, right?"

Tessa couldn't deny it, so she remained silent.

Ben let out an annoyed sigh. "She's wrong. I had nothing to do with it." He shook his head. "She's only got herself to blame." He finished wiping the kitchen bench before turning and meeting Tessa's gaze. "I guess she won't want me at her graduation if she thinks like that?"

"Not at all. She needs our support more than ever. If you don't go, it'll just make her believe it was you. I don't think she believes you'd do something like that, it's just her way of coping with the shock. She's lashing out at whoever she can."

As Ben fixed his eyes on her, Tessa's heart fell. She hated the underlying tension that had existed between the two of them ever since she'd told Ben about Michael's email. And now, she got the feeling he didn't accept what she'd said, and that she also believed it was him who'd betrayed Stephanie.

With the uncomfortable tension with Ben still floating in the air, she thought it best to stay home, so she phoned Stephanie instead. Hannah answered and said Stephanie was asleep. Tessa breathed a sigh of relief, although she felt a little guilty at doing so. She prayed silently for her, asking God to work something good in all of this, and joined Ben on the couch.

Stephanie's graduation ceremony was scheduled for that Friday night at the Southbank Convention Centre. Tessa doubted Ben would end up going, but she'd convinced him it was the right thing to do, and she took his hand as he sat beside her in the huge auditorium. Stephanie's mother had at the last minute been unable to come due to an emergency on the farm. Stephanie had said she was relieved in one way. It gave her more time before having to admit her failure.

Throughout the whole of the ceremony, Stephanie stared at her hands, only looking up when her name was called. Her gaze was vacant as she walked onto the stage to receive her certificate. Seeing her like this tore at Tessa's heart.

Stephanie's cheeks were tear-stained when they met up after the ceremony. Tessa threw her arms around her neck and hugged her tightly. "It'll be okay, Steph, you'll see. Chin up."

Stephanie forced a smile and wiped her cheeks.

Tessa urged Ben forward. Stephanie held her body rigid

and lifted her chin as he leaned forward and kissed her on the cheek.

"I don't know how to make you believe me. It wasn't me who told on you, and I have no idea who did." Tessa's heart warmed at the softness in his voice. He really was trying.

"I can't think of anyone else who would have." Defeat hung heavily in Stephanie voice. "It doesn't matter now. I'm sure you think I deserve it."

Ben shook his head. "You're wrong. I only want the best for you, believe it or not."

"What are you going to do now, Steph?" Tessa asked, trying to diffuse the situation.

Stephanie turned and shrugged dejectedly. "I don't know. I think I'll spend a few weeks with my mum on the farm. Being away from everything for a while might help clear my head."

Tessa smiled warmly at her and hugged her tightly. "Don't be disheartened. Stay strong. And remember, God is with you."

CHAPTER 14

With Stephanie about to go away, Tessa was more eager than ever to form a friendship with Margaret Smith. She needed another woman to talk with, even if Margaret was a little older. In fact, she could have been her mother. Tessa figured that could be a good thing. Margaret had raised three children, so perhaps she could give some advice regarding Jayden. She'd been reading the books on step-parenting Stephanie had given her, but it wouldn't hurt to get some real life know-how on raising a teenager.

Margaret didn't live too far away. When Tessa drove up for their agreed upon lunch date, she was in the front yard snipping the dead heads off the rose bushes lining her front fence.

"Welcome to my humble abode," she said, greeting Tessa warmly. She removed her old gardening gloves and led the way inside. "Come right on in." The living room was spotless. A large colourful mat sat in the middle of the dark timber floor, surrounded by a lounge suite, which although old and well used, still looked inviting and comfortable. Photos, which Tessa guessed were of family members, stood in fancy frames on top of the mantelpiece, and white chandelier light fittings adorned the extra high ceiling.

"I love your house. It's so quaint and oldie worldy. It's lovely." Tessa smiled warmly at the older woman.

"Thank you. I must admit to quite liking it myself." Margaret chuckled. "We've lived here all our married life, so it holds a lot of memories."

She headed into the kitchen, but not before tossing her wide-brimmed floppy sun hat onto a chair as she passed by. "Silly me, always forgetting to take this off in the house." Margaret's chatty, good-natured personality made Tessa smile. After putting the water on for tea, she rejoined Tessa in the living room. "I'm truly glad you could come. I always enjoy getting to know new folks."

"Thank you for asking me." Tessa pointed to the framed photos. "Your family?"

"Ah, yes." Margaret picked up each one in turn. "This is my husband, Harold. We've been married forty years next year. And these are our two daughters, Chloe and Sophie. They're twins—you can probably tell just by looking at them, and you'll never believe this—they went and married twin brothers!"

"Really?" Tessa laughed.

Margaret chuckled and nodded. "They're all in London now, and I'm worried I won't be able to tell my grandbabies apart when I see them next." She picked up the last photo and her smiled faded. "And here's Harrison, my baby."

Tessa leaned closer. *Harrison?* Not Harrison who worked

for her, surely? She peered closer still. Although considerably younger in the photo, it was him, no question about it. His high cheekbones, big brown eyes and jet black hair confirmed it.

"Harrison works for me. I had no idea."

Margaret blinked. "Really? I didn't know you were a vet." Something about Margaret's expression wasn't right.

"Yes—I'm Practice Manager at the moment, although I'd love to be back doing hands on work. It's a small world, isn't it?" Tessa stepped back a little. Margaret stared wistfully at the photo for a second longer before replacing it. What was going on here? Surely it was the twins Margaret was missing; Harrison lived nearby.

"Yes, it is," she said in a faraway voice, but then her expression lightened. "What about you, Tessa? Do you have children?" Before she could answer, Margaret touched her arm lightly. "I'm sorry. I just remembered you told me you were recently married."

"Yes, I am, but Ben's son lives with us. So yes, I do have a child—actually, I have a teenager..." Tessa blew out a slow breath. "And he's really testing me out, I'm afraid."

Margaret chuckled, her face lighting up. "Teenagers have a habit of doing that."

The kettle began to whistle. "Come on, it's time for lunch." Margaret hurried into the kitchen and filled a red china teapot with steaming water. She indicated to Tessa to take a seat and gave thanks for the food. Uncovering a plate of dainty sandwiches, she encouraged Tessa to take as many as she liked. Tessa chose an egg and lettuce sandwich and also a chicken and salad, and placed both on her plate, but all of a sudden she didn't feel like eating. In fact, the smell of the egg made her nauseous. Not wanting to be rude, she nibbled the chicken sandwich. As she chewed, she thought about Margaret's behaviour. Something wasn't quite right. But dare she ask? She'd hoped Margaret might give her some input with how to handle Jayden. She had no thought it might be Margaret who needed help.

Tessa washed the sandwich down with a sip of tea and then decided to ask. She cleared her throat. "Is everything all right between you and Harrison?"

Margaret's face fell and for a long moment she said nothing. She twisted her tea cup between her hands before smiling rather sadly. "Harrison doesn't talk to me anymore. We haven't seen each other since he left school, and that was a long time ago."

"But why? You live so close." Tessa's brow furrowed. How could anyone, let alone her son, not want to see this sweet, kind woman? Tessa leaned forward in her chair and gazed sympathetically at Margaret.

Margaret sighed deeply. "It's a long story."

"It's okay, I'm happy to listen." Tessa smiled encouragingly.

"Okay, thanks. Stop me if you want." Margaret drew in a deep breath and began. "When I was growing up, my parents struggled with money and we were poor my entire childhood." She wrapped her hands tightly around her cup. "I was determined to make a better life for myself, so I studied hard and became a journalist. When I met Harold, I had a high-paying job with a woman's magazine. After we married, Harold was more than happy for me to keep working, even when the children came along. He understood my need to give the children a better life than what I'd had growing up."

Margaret bit her lip and stared into her cup, a pained expression growing on her face. "The job required me to travel a lot. I missed more birthdays and rugby practices and school events than I should have. Harrison was always asking where I was or why I couldn't watch him, and then one day he just stopped asking and didn't want anything more to do with me." Margaret's eyes misted over. Tessa reached out and lightly touched her arm. "He had everything he needed, apart from a mother who was there for him." She lifted a tissue to her eyes and looked up. "I deeply regret not spending more time with him and the girls. If I could go back and change things, I would, but at the time, I thought I was doing the right thing."

Tessa sat quietly, digesting all that Margaret had said. Her honesty and desire to give her children a better life was touching. Listening to her, the thought came to Tessa that behind many a happy facade lay a sad story. *Even my own mother had a sad story she'd kept secret for years.* The thought didn't alleviate Tessa's concerns over her situation with Jayden, but it provided comfort to know she wasn't alone. Others had their unique set of problems they faced daily, and it was unrealistic of her to expect that her life would be free of challenges.

But how unfair that Harrison couldn't see his mother had acted out of love. Another thought came to her—*maybe that's why he's giving me such a hard time—he thinks I should be a stay-at-home mother.* She cocked her head and drew her eyebrows together. *Surely not, not in this day and age? Every mother works, don't they?*

Tessa met Margaret's questioning gaze. "I was just thinking that might explain why Harrison doesn't like me as his boss."

Margaret's eyes watered again. "I'm sorry if he treats you badly. I'm to blame for that."

Tessa reached across the table and grasped Margaret's hand. "No. Parents make mistakes, but when children become adults they have to take responsibility for their own behaviour. Your daughters didn't turn out like Harrison, did they?"

A smile came to the older woman's face. "No, thank God. They were always proud of my work. We talk over the phone every week and Harold and I are going to visit them in London during the winter." Her expression faded. "But Harrison, well, I guess boys take things differently." She sighed and took a sip of tea before drawing her eyebrows together. "You've barely touched your sandwich. Can I get you something else?"

Tessa looked down at her plate. It was true. She'd only nibbled one sandwich, but the thought of eating any more made her stomach turn. Strange, because she normally liked sandwiches.

"No, thank you. That's very kind. The sandwiches are lovely, but I just don't seem to be very hungry." As she spoke, her stomach convulsed and rose to her throat. She covered her mouth with her hand. "I'm sorry, I think I'm going to be sick."

Margaret's eyes widened. She hopped up and grabbed a bowl off the sink. "Here, take this." She handed Tessa the bowl, just in time for her to heave her entire breakfast, morning tea and lunch into it.

"I'm so sorry." She quickly looked up before heaving again. When there was no more left to bring up, she took the towel

Margaret offered and wiped her face. "I'm not sure what came over me. I feel so embarrassed."

"Don't you worry about that." Margaret took her by the arm and led her to a couch in the living room. She went back to the kitchen and returned with a glass of cold water. Tessa sipped it thankfully.

"Have you been to a doctor lately?"

Tessa shook her head.

"I think you should go see one." Margaret sat on the couch alongside her and leaned forward, eyes glowing.

"I'm sure it's nothing." Tessa took another sip of water.

"You don't understand." Margaret touched her lightly on her wrist. "Lack of appetite, feeling nauseous and lightheadedness are all symptoms of pregnancy."

Tessa's eyed widened. *Pregnancy? No, I can't be pregnant...* She straightened until she was sitting on the edge of the couch. She glanced down at her flat stomach and then back at Margaret. "I can't be. We've been taking precautions." Her pulse began to race.

"I've been through it twice and I think I can tell, but you should see your doctor to be absolutely certain." Margaret eyes twinkled as Tessa's mind worked overtime. *Pregnant?* She and Ben had been planning on having children in the future, but not yet. It was too soon. She wasn't ready. *Or was she?*

On the way home from Margaret's, Tessa was in a daze, unable to believe Margaret's theory for her sudden bout of vomiting until she realised she hadn't had a period since before their honeymoon. She'd been so busy since returning that she hadn't noticed—until now. The realisation sent her into a panic. Her heart skipped a beat and her face grew warm. *Maybe Margaret was right after all.* She pulled over at the first pharmacy she passed and picked up a pregnancy test kit. There was one way to find out.

CHAPTER 15

"Tessa, is this what I think it is?" Ben emerged from the bathroom carrying a white stick with a quizzical look on his face.

Tessa chastised herself. She'd meant to throw it away but her mind had drifted to Michael's email again when she was showering and she'd forgotten about it.

"Sorry. I meant to throw it away. I threw up at lunch and Margaret had a strange thought I might be pregnant, so I picked up a test kit on the way home. She was wrong, just as I'd expected. I must have eaten something bad." She stepped into the bathroom and squeezed toothpaste onto her brush. Despite rinsing many times at Margaret's, her mouth still tasted of vomit. Maybe it was her imagination, but a good clean would fix it either way.

Ben followed her and she caught his reflection in the mirror. A deep frown sat on his forehead. He still held the stick in his hand. "But it's positive."

Her mouth fell open as she stopped mid brush. She quickly spat into the basin and turned around. "It can't be, I checked. It was negative."

"It looks positive to me."

She stared at the stick in his hand. He was right. How had she gotten it wrong? Her heart went into a flap.

Ben took her hands. "Tessa, look at me."

She lifted her gaze and stared at him. She couldn't take this in.

"This is wonderful news. We're having a baby!" His eyes shone with excitement. She'd never seen him so animated.

"But we hadn't planned it." Her chest tightened and she struggled to breathe.

"If God has decided to bless us with a baby, who are we to argue?"

She searched his eyes as the reality of what could be began to take hold deep inside her. "Are you sure? You said we should wait a year." Her voice was breathless and she swallowed the lump in her throat. Could she really be pregnant?

"Yes, I'm sure. This is the best thing that's happened to me. I'm so excited." He pulled her close and pressed his lips against her hair.

She leaned back and angled her head. "The best thing?"

"Well, apart from marrying you, that is."

She gazed into his eyes as love for him flooded through her veins. All thoughts of Michael fled her mind. "And marrying you is the best thing that's happened to me, and having your baby is, well, it's overwhelming." Tears pricked her eyes. "I still can't believe it. I think I need some time to take it in."

"Take as long as you want." He brushed her hair lightly with his fingers and gazed into her eyes. "It might not be what we planned, but we need to thank God for His blessings. Children are a gift from God, and I'm so thankful for Him blessing us like this."

A moment of silence passed between them. He was right. Children were definitely a gift from God, and instead of being anxious, she should be grateful. But was she ready to be a mother to a baby *and* a teenager? Her heart raced again. *Jayden. How will he handle the news?* She asked Ben what he thought.

"I hope he'll be happy, but who knows with Jayden? Up one minute, down the next." Ben lifted her chin as he continued gazing into her eyes. "We'll just have to trust God to work it out."

She drew in a long breath and nodded. Not only would they need to trust God to work it out in Jayden's life, she'd need to trust God to work it out in her own. Being pregnant was definitely an unexpected turn of events. She closed her eyes and rested her head against Ben's shoulder as he held her tightly. *God, I need You more than ever right now. Be my strength and fortress, and help me be the best mother I can be, to both this little baby and to Jayden.*

TESSA MADE an appointment with the doctor for Monday afternoon after work. Her pregnancy was confirmed. She was six weeks, and the doctor said she was in excellent health and should have a normal pregnancy, and that it wasn't that uncommon to fall pregnant whilst taking birth control pills.

Her stomach was full of butterflies as she left the surgery. Although she'd had two days to prepare herself for this news, having the doctor confirm she was indeed carrying a brand new life inside her made it all the more real, and a thousand thoughts scurried through her mind causing her to heart to race.

Seated in her car, she placed her hand on her tummy and settled her breathing. *I really am having a baby.* The truth of the matter finally sank in and she let out a slow breath as she smiled to herself. "Lord, this really is so unexpected, and I'm sorry for my initial reaction. Now it's confirmed, I'm excited to be having a baby. Thank You for your infinite blessings, and thank You for this wonderful gift." Warmth flowed from her heart and spread through her body. "I'm not sure I'm ready to be a mother to a teenager and a baby, Lord, but I trust You to be with me the whole way. Bless this little baby, and help Ben and me to be the best parents ever. Thank You, Lord." Her voice choked and tears filled her eyes. She dabbed the tears with a tissue and then lowered her gaze to her stomach. "Now to tell your daddy…"

WHEN BEN WALKED in the door not long after Tessa, he had a spring to his step and an expectant look on his face.

Tessa stood in the hallway with a playful grin on her face. "The doctor confirmed it. We're having a baby!"

A huge smile split his face as he whipped a bunch of brightly coloured flowers from behind his back and presented them to her. He wrapped his free arm around her and pressed his lips to her forehead.

"That is the best news." His eyes glistened and the smile on his face stretched from ear to ear.

"I know. It really is." Her voice caught in her throat. Now she'd gotten used to the idea of being pregnant, giving Ben a child so soon after their wedding filled her with a great sense of joy, especially knowing how much he'd longed for more children in his first marriage—he'd been denied that pleasure by Kathryn's selfishness. It didn't matter that it had happened earlier than planned; it was exciting and she would embrace the journey. She leaned her head against his shoulder, and his arm closed around her waist, pulling her close. She'd never felt so loved in all her life.

As she placed the flowers into a vase a short while later, she told him what the doctor had said. "Everything is fine, but she suggested we not tell anyone for a while, just in case."

Ben's brows came together. "Does she think something might be wrong?"

"No, she just said it's early days, and it was only a suggestion."

He let out a relieved sigh. "Nothing's going to happen, but if you want to wait a while to tell everyone, that's okay. It can be our secret for now." He stepped closer and embraced her once more.

He insisted she rest in the living room while he and Jayden cooked dinner.

"But why? I'm not sick, just preg..." She clamped her hand to her mouth, her eyes springing open. *Had Jayden heard?* She slowly turned her head to where he sat in the family room, engrossed in a television programme. She turned her head back to Ben. "Phew, that was close." She rolled her eyes and let out a small chuckle.

"We're not going to be able to keep it from him for long,

you know. Maybe we should tell him now." Ben slid his arm around her waist and pulled her close. He was paying her so much attention it made her laugh.

Her face straightened. Would it hurt to tell Jayden now? Maybe he'd appreciate being part of the secret. "If you think we should tell him, it's okay with me."

"Let's tell him over dinner." Ben kissed the top of her head before letting her go. "Come on, show me what to do."

Tessa shook her head and laughed. "One day you'll learn to cook, Ben Williams."

A short while later, as the three of them sat down to a chicken stir fry Ben had helped her make, Tessa leapt up and raced for the bathroom, making it just in time. After heaving up all the contents of her stomach, she stood slowly and looked in the mirror. Her face had paled and her hair hung limply against her cheeks. If they hadn't decided to tell Jayden already, he'd certainly be asking questions now. She splashed her face with cold water and rinsed her mouth. So much for morning sickness. What about evening sickness? Nobody had told her about that.

"I'm sorry," she said when she returned to the table. Ben reached out and squeezed her hand. She met his gaze and nodded. He cleared his throat.

Jayden lifted his head, looking first at his father and then at her.

"Jayden, we have some news for you." Ben paused and squeezed her hand again. His eyes glistened, causing her to push back tears of her own. *Oh God, please help Jayden to take this okay.* Her heart beat faster as she glanced at his suspicious expression.

His eyes narrowed. "Well, what is it?"

"We're having a baby. You're going to have a little brother or sister before the end of the year." A large grin split Ben's face, but slowly faded as Jayden's eyes darkened.

Jayden folded his arms and glared at his father.

Tessa touched his arm gently. "A baby isn't going to change anything. Your dad and I both love you dearly. You might not believe it, but it's the truth."

Ben leaned forward. "Tessa's right. Having a baby isn't going to change anything between us."

"Yeah right." Jayden rolled his eyes to the ceiling before sliding further down in his chair. "I bet the camping trip's off."

"Absolutely not." Tessa straightened. "In fact, we're picking the gear up after your football game on Saturday. Isn't that right, Ben?" She willed him to support her, and to be sensitive to Jayden's needs at this pivotal time.

"Ah, yes, that's right. It's all happening. I'll talk to Neil's parents on the weekend to make sure they're still okay with him coming. So, the camping trip is definitely on. As Tessa told me in no uncertain words a little earlier, she's not sick, she's just pregnant."

She caught his gaze and gave him an approving smile.

"So, you see, a baby isn't going to alter anything, and your dad and I are sure you're going to be a fantastic big brother when he or she comes along." Tessa touched his arm again lightly, and smiled into his eyes, trying to draw him out of his negativity. "Come on—everything is going to be all right."

Jayden shrugged one shoulder and picked up his fork.

Tessa's heart went out to him—no doubt he felt threatened

by the news. She and Ben would just have to convince him that their assurances were sincere and genuine.

Having a baby wouldn't change anything between them.

She picked up a tiny piece of chicken and popped it tentatively into her mouth. It was going to be a long nine months.

CHAPTER 16

Late the following Saturday morning, Ben and Tessa sat under a row of shady gumtrees bordering the football field where Jayden's team was about to play. Tessa sipped her coffee as she gazed about. Beside her, Ben flipped through the Financial Times. She had no idea how he could read such a boring newspaper.

She'd been thinking about their visit to her parents' place after the game all morning. Several weeks had passed since their last visit, and she wondered if her mother, being naturally intuitive, would notice anything different about her without being told. It wouldn't be a surprise if she did. Tessa let out a slow breath. *Maybe we should just tell them.* She turned to Ben and voiced her thoughts.

Lifting his head from the newspaper, he gave her a puzzled look. "I thought you wanted to wait?"

"Well, I did, but Mum will probably notice anyway, so I'm thinking we should."

"Your decision, my sweet. As long as you're happy about it, it's fine by me." He folded the newspaper neatly and placed it in his backpack. "I'm sure they'll be thrilled."

She gave a soft laugh. "Yes, they will. First grandchild and all." Her laugh fell flat. "Sorry. That was thoughtless. I'm not used to thinking of Jayden as their grandson, but I need to."

"It's okay." He squeezed her hand and smiled reassuringly. Leaning in close, he whispered, "Just don't say it in front of Jayden." His eyes glinted mischievously.

Tessa hit him playfully. "I won't. Look, here they come." She pointed to the team of boys running onto the field. Jayden, with the number ten on the back of his blue and red striped jersey, glanced their way and she stood and waved without thinking.

Ben tugged her shirt, pulling her back to her seat. "Not sure he'd want you to do that."

She hung her head in mock shame. "Have I messed up again?"

Ben chuckled. "I think he'll forgive you. At least we're here, watching. He can't complain about that."

Not long into the game, Jayden was passed the ball ten metres from the try line. She and Ben both jumped out their seats and held their breath. Jayden fumbled but then pulled the ball in, tucking it under his arm as he sprinted towards the line. He slid into touch as two much heavier boys from the opposing team made a lunge for him.

"That's my boy!" Ben thrust his arm into the air and yelled. Tessa stared at him, laughing. She'd never seen or heard him so excited.

Jayden couldn't wipe the smile off his face as his team

mates congratulated him for scoring the first try of the match.

The team went on to win by fifteen points, but Jayden saw no further action. Tessa expected him to be the star of the team, but it seemed his one and only try was just that. A one and only. Every time he was passed the ball, he dropped it, and his team mates stopped passing to him. He fumbled any tackle he attempted, and eventually the coach benched him.

Ben sighed and lost interest in the game, returning to his Financial Times. Tessa kept glancing at Jayden as he sat on the bench with a dejected look on his face, kicking the dirt below with the toe of his boot. Her heart went out to him. She recalled the words he spoke to her not so long ago: *"Dad played rugby when he was in school, and he was good at it. He won a lot of awards. He'd be disappointed if I didn't play."*

Maybe he doesn't want to play after all but isn't game to tell his dad. Poor Jayden.

On the way to her parents' place, she tried to make light of it, but neither Ben nor Jayden responded to her attempts at conversation and she finally gave up and looked out the window. She hoped Ben would be more sensitive with the new baby than he was with Jayden.

When they announced their news over lunch, Eleanor jumped up and hugged Tessa and Telford clapped Ben on the back.

"I must admit I did suspect," her mother said as she hugged Tessa tightly. "We'll have to go shopping for maternity clothes, and we can look for baby items at the same time. I know it's early, but it never hurts to plan."

"Slow down, Mum, I'm not even showing yet! But a shopping trip would be lovely." Her mother would most likely want her to wear those old fashioned maternity dresses that made expectant mothers look like elephants, but it didn't matter. It'd been too long since she and her mother had spent any quality time together, and she would look forward to the outing, even if they disagreed on what clothes to buy.

Tessa stood and began collecting the dirty lunch plates. "Don't forget we're also picking up the camping gear. Dad, do you want to take Ben and Jayden into the shed and sort it?"

"Well, that's a not too subtle way of being told you're not wanted!" Her father laughed his big laugh, his bushy eyebrows bobbing up and down above his heavily creased eyes, but he rose anyway. Ben and Jayden followed him outside.

Over the dishes, Eleanor asked Tessa how she was coping with everything. "I know you're pregnant, but I can sense when you have things on your mind."

Tessa sighed and looked her mother in the eye. "How do you do it, Mum? How do you just *know?*"

Eleanor stopped washing and dried her hands on her apron. "All I can say is that God has given me the gift of discernment, and I can often see below the surface and know when things aren't quite right. Not always, but often." She reached out and took Tessa's hand. "So, what's troubling you, my precious one? Is it Ben, or is it Jayden? Or is it someone else?"

That was a good question. If she were honest, she'd have to say it was both Ben and Jayden, although things with the two of them had settled down some, and she was learning to accept Ben's fussy ways, although she doubted she'd ever accept his strictness with Jayden. But it wasn't just them. It was work; it was Harrison and Margaret; it was Sabrina; it was Stephanie; it was Michael. Tessa's shoulders fell. *Michael.* She still hadn't given him an answer and he'd be in Brisbane this week.

She wrung her hands. "It's a whole lot of things, and I don't know where to start." *Or how much I should say...*

"Let's have a cup of tea, and start wherever you want."

Tessa sat with her mother and told her about Margaret and Harrison, and how sad it was that Harrison refused to see his mother even though she'd been trying to make amends for such a long time. "You were a stay-at-home mother. Do you think it's wrong for mothers to work?"

"That was a long time ago, sweetheart. Things have changed, and it's normal for most mothers to work, but back then, your father and I made the decision that caring for the family would be my main priority, and that we'd go without some of the luxuries we'd otherwise have. Your friend Margaret made the other choice, and it seems she's still paying the price for it. But I can't say if it's right or wrong. It's something you and Ben have to work through together. I'm guessing that's what you're getting at. Am I right?"

Tessa nodded. "Yes, of course you're right." She rested her forearms on the table, her hands wrapped around her tea-cup. "I'm not really enjoying being manager." She drew in a deep breath. "I'd love to go back to my old job, but I don't think Fran would be happy with that, especially when she finds out I'm pregnant."

"You can learn a lot by seeing things through, and I'm sure Fran will be flexible if you decide to return to work after a decent break." Eleanor placed her hand lightly on Tessa's arm.

"Talk to Ben about it, dear, and pray about it. But don't give in just because it's too hard. It's good to be challenged sometimes, and you never know, God might have placed you in that position to help build the bridge between Harrison and his mum.

Exactly what she'd been thinking, but not necessarily what she wanted to hear. *Maybe I do run when things get too hard, like Sabrina said. Like with Michael...*

Tessa shifted her gaze to her tea-cup and inhaled slowly. What would her mother say to this one? She cocked her head slightly. "Michael's back in town. He's been in rehab, and he's recommitted his life to Jesus."

Her mother's immediate response was to smile. "That's great news, sweetheart." But her smile was soon replaced with a concerned expression as she studied her daughter. "What's the matter?" She leaned forward and touched Tessa's arm lightly.

Tessa levelled her gaze at her mother. "He wants to see me."

"Oh." Her mother sat back and drew a breath.

Tessa pinched her bottom lip. "Ben doesn't want me to see him."

Eleanor held her daughter's gaze. "I can understand that. I imagine Ben's threatened by Michael, especially after what happened with his first wife."

"Yes, I know, but this is different. It's not like I'm going to run off with Michael or anything. I'm just annoyed that Ben doesn't seem to trust me."

Her mother leaned back. "Why do you want to see him?"

Tessa inhaled slowly. "Just to clear the air between us. I still care about him, and I feel bad about how it all ended." Her eyes misted over.

"Yes, but if it's causing problems between you and Ben, don't go. Ben's your priority now, not Michael, regardless of how you feel."

Tessa bit her lip and looked out the window. "I had a feeling you'd say that."

Before her mother could ask any more questions, the boys stomped up the stairs and entered the kitchen, filling it with their chatter.

"I think we got everything out, but you can check if you want." Her father chuckled. "It's all pretty old. Hasn't been used since your mother and I went on that road trip about eight years ago, but it should be in good order."

"Everything of yours is in good order." Tessa laughed lightly, brushing away her concerns over Michael for now.

"We pulled out that old tent of yours, too. Hopefully it'll be all right for the two boys. Might pay to check it."

"What you're saying is that because it's mine it might not be in good order?" Tessa raised her brows playfully.

"Well…"

"Telford, that's enough!" Eleanor reached back and tapped her husband's hands. Although she sounded serious, there was an underlying warmth to her voice.

"We'll check it, Dad. It's okay." Tessa let out a resigned sigh.

"Have you been camping before, Jayden?" Eleanor turned and looked at Jayden who'd been hanging back behind both Telford and Ben. She grabbed his hand and drew him down onto the seat beside her.

"I used to go camping often when I was in scouts, but I haven't been since then." He flashed an accusing look at his father. "Dad doesn't like camping."

"That's not true. I've just never been." Ben's face reddened.

Tessa slipped her hand into his. "But we're going next weekend. And we're going to have a great time, aren't we?" She gazed up into his eyes, willing him to be encouraging for Jayden's sake.

Ben drew in a slow breath. "Yes, we're going to have a great time." His voice sounded a little strained, but at least he was trying.

As they said their good-byes a short while later, Eleanor took Tessa's hands in hers. "I have no doubt you'll be a wonderful mother. Seems like just yesterday I was welcoming you into the world, but now you're all grown up with a family of your own and it's your turn to bring a daughter or son into the world." Her eyes moistened, and Tessa's eyes blurred with tears of her own. "Being a mother is exhausting and wonderful—the greatest thing that can happen to you, but it can also be the most challenging. I have no doubt God will give you all the grace, strength, and wisdom you'll need to love and raise your child the way he wants you to." Her mother's voice was warm and soft, and she had a tear in her eye. She reached out and brushed a stray hair from Tessa's forehead. "I'll be praying for you at every stage of your journey, honey. You can count on that."

Fresh tears pricked Tessa's eyes as her mother hugged her tightly and planted a big kiss on her cheek.

"Thanks Mum, I appreciate that." Tessa smiled into her mother's watery eyes, her voice catching in her throat. "And I'll look forward to that shopping trip." She squeezed her hand before letting go and climbing into the front passenger seat beside Ben.

CHAPTER 17

Eleanor's words weighed on Tessa's mind all the way home. *"If it's causing problems between you and Ben, don't go..."* She glanced at Ben in the driver's seat. The day out had done him good. He seemed more relaxed, despite the prospect of the camping trip and Jayden's disappointing performance that morning. But if she mentioned Michael's name, tension would reappear, and she didn't want that at all. The more she thought about it, the more she believed she would need to put aside her desire to see Michael for the benefit of her marriage. But Michael still needed a response. It was unfair to leave him hanging like she had, and as he was due to arrive this week, time was running out.

Long shadows extended to the other side of the road by the time they arrived home. Ben and Jayden unpacked the camping gear and stacked it on several shelves in the carport, ready to be repacked the following weekend. Jayden disappeared into his room, and Ben was keen to watch the football game on television between the Brisbane Broncos and the North Queensland Cowboys, as long as she didn't mind. She didn't mind at all. It gave her the perfect opportunity to draft an email to Michael.

SHE KNEW the contents of Michael's email by heart. Countless times she'd pictured him sitting on a chair as he wrote it, full of hope that she might be willing to rekindle their friendship. Now she had to dash his dreams. *God, I feel so bad. I don't know what to write, please help me.* She drew in a deep breath and, placing her fingers on the keyboard, began.

'Dear Michael,

Please forgive me for not replying to your welcome email sooner. I was so glad to hear about your successful rehabilitation, and even gladder to hear about your re-commitment to the Lord.'

She paused, reading over what she'd just written. Did it sound too stuffy and formal? *Probably—but best to keep going or I'll never finish it.*

'I do have news to tell you of my own. I have no idea of your sister's motivation for not telling you herself, as she is obviously aware of it. I can only think she wanted to cause strife for me as she's never held any great love for me, especially after you and I parted ways. Michael, I have to tell you that I'm now married. I hope that doesn't come as too much of a shock. I know you were hoping to rekindle our friendship, but at this early stage in my marriage, I don't believe I can be more than someone you once knew, and possibly loved.

What we had was wonderful while it lasted, and I have many treasured memories of our time together. When I think back to our happy times, it makes the unhappy times so much sadder. I'll never forget the day of your accident, the day everything changed. You were in so much pain, and my heart went out to you as you lay in that hospital bed with goodness knows how many tubes and monitors poking into and out of you. And the devastating news that you might never be able to do any active sports again. I know how difficult that was for you, as our lives were filled with so many fun activities, and the prospect of never being able to scuba dive or ski again, or even ride your bike, I think probably caused you to get hooked on those drugs. They not only eased your physical pain, but also helped you forget about your loss.

I tried to understand that at the time, but maybe I wasn't mature enough to know how to really help you. I thought it was just a simple matter of accepting the situation, praying about it and getting on with life, but now I realise that emotional healing often takes longer, and I needed to be more patient and caring. I'm sorry I failed you, I truly am. However, what happened can't be undone. It can only be remembered as a time when we both struggled, and sadly ended with us parting ways. I hope you'll forgive me for choosing to go my own way, and for leaving you to deal with your problems on your own. At the time, I felt I could do nothing more, despite praying for your healing and hoping God would help you get off those drugs.

I guess you're wondering who I married. Before I tell you, let me assure you it took a long time for me to face life again without you. Just ask Stephanie! She often had to drag me out of bed to go to work, and so often I wanted to call you and say I was sorry I'd broken it off, but I didn't, and I slowly rebuilt my life without you in it. And then, one day, actually, it was one night, when I was at puppy training (yes, I now have a dog—I found him in the car park at work and brought him home), I met this wonderful man. I was hesitant to get involved at first, mainly because he's a bit older than me and has a teenage son, but we slowly fell in love. He's a deep thinker, and was suffering from depression when we met after his wife walked out on him, but he's a Christian and he's a deeply caring man, and I love with all my heart. We married in January, and moved into a new house in New Farm—all three of us. Can you imagine me as a stepmother to a teenager? I couldn't for a long time, but God has given me a real love for Jayden, and even though we struggle in our relationship sometimes (often, if I'm honest), I think we're doing all right.'

She paused again. *Should I tell him I'm pregnant?* She tapped the desk and inhaled slowly, and eventually decided against it. No need.

'I can't say enough how happy I am that your rehab was successful. But what makes me happier still is your re-commitment to the Lord. I pray that in the weeks and months to come, your faith will grow stronger every day, and you'll find peace and fulfilment in your life because Jesus is living in your heart. No doubt there will be dark days when temptation comes your way, but stay strong in the Lord and don't give in. When you're weak, then He is strong. Pray often and immerse yourself in the Word, and surround yourself with others who love Jesus. I'm sorry I'm sounding like a preacher—I don't mean it to sound like that. In fact, I've just re-read what I wrote, and I need to take my own advice!

Anyway, in conclusion, I just want to say that I wish you all of God's best for the future. I pray that He'll lead and guide you, and that you will find direction in your life. I hope that one day we can meet again, but until then, please be assured of my deep affection.

Tessa'

. . .

TESSA EXHALED SLOWLY and closed her eyes as she leaned back in her chair. Was she ready to hit the send button? How would Michael react when he received it? Had she come on too heavy? She took a deep breath. *God, please bless this email, and prepare Michael's heart. Wrap him in your love, and protect him from the disappointment he might feel when he receives it. And Lord, please help him to grow strong in you, and become the man of God you want him to be. And lastly, Lord, please help me to grow closer to you, too. I'm sorry for my stubbornness and the way I've treated Ben just because I wanted my own way. Please forgive me. Amen.*

She straightened herself and without any more ado, hit the 'send' button.

TESSA WAS sure Michael would always hold a special place in her heart, but Ben was the love of her life, the one she'd promised God she'd love through sickness and health, through bad times and good, and now she needed to tell him she wasn't going to see Michael.

CHAPTER 18

Tessa stretched and glanced at the clock. She'd been at her computer longer than she thought. Strange the boys hadn't been calling for dinner. She closed her computer down and ran her hands over her tummy. A sense of warmth and God's peace settled over her now she'd done what she knew was the right thing.

When she stepped into the living room, Ben was asleep on the couch looking very peaceful. The football game had finished and the news was on. She tip-toed to the television to lower the volume, but just as she reached it, Ben stirred. She turned around and smiled at him. "Enjoy the game, sweetie?"

Clearing his throat, he pulled himself upright and yawned. "Ah, yes, it was a close game." His brows pinched as he peered at his watch. "How long have I been asleep?"

"Not long. The news has just started. Is Jayden still in his room?"

Ben glanced up the stairs. "As far as I know. He said he needed to study, but that was a while ago."

"Are you sure he's studying?" Tessa arched her brows as she joined Ben on the couch.

He placed his arm around her and kissed her cheek. "That's what he said. I don't think he'd lie."

"I'm not saying he's lying, but there are a thousand other things for kids to do on the computer besides studying. It might be worth checking."

"I guess you're right. I'll go check in a minute." He straightened and began gently massaging her shoulders. "So what has Mrs. Williams been up to while her husband has been lazing in front of the television?"

She sighed. How much should she tell him? No doubt he'd be happy about her decision not to see Michael, but the finality of it all still saddened her a little. She wondered if Michael had already read the email, and as she did, her heart raced at she thought of him opening it. *God, I've already prayed about this, but please wrap your arms around Michael right now. It's going to be such a shock for him.* Ben began massaging her neck, and she remembered he was waiting for an answer. She breathed in slowly and squeezed her hands together. "I sent an email to Michael."

Ben stopped his massaging and his body stiffened. "What did you say?" The tone of his voice suggested he was expecting the worst.

She turned her head and met his gaze. For a long moment they remained that way, neither of them moving or breathing. She inhaled deeply. "I told him I won't be able to see him."

Ben's body visibly relaxed. He took her hand. "I'm so glad you made that decision. I'd been wondering, and hoping."

"I'm sorry I took so long." She squeezed his hands. "You deserved an answer long before now, but it's done now. I won't be seeing him."

"What made you decide?" Ben's voice had softened, and as he gazed into her eyes, she knew she'd made the right decision. Ben might not be as fun loving as Michael had been, but he was solid and steady, and he loved her deeply. Her heart warmed as he brushed his finger slowly along her brow.

"I realised how much you mean to me, and how selfish of me to want to see him." She paused and drew a deep breath. "I should have made the decision straight away instead of toying with the idea for so long. I think I was being just a little stubborn, too. I'm so sorry."

A moment of silence passed between them. Tessa's heart beat faster when Ben lifted her chin and caressed her face as he did.

"I was so scared of losing you." His voice caught in his throat.

Tears pricked her eyes and tumbled down her cheeks.

Ben wiped them gently with his thumbs, and then pulled her closer until their lips met in a kiss that left her in no doubt of his love and forgiveness.

HALF AN HOUR LATER, Ben went up to Jayden's bedroom to tell him dinner was ready. Instead of hearing the rock music that would normally be playing, all was quiet. When he opened the door, Jayden jumped at the sudden interruption.

"What are you up to?" Ben stepped closer and tried to look, but it was too late. Jayden slammed his MacBook Air shut.

"Studying."

"Really?"

"Yes. We've got a big algebra test next week. Most of the class is still struggling with some of the formulae, so the teacher set up a group on Facebook that lets us chat with one another if we need help."

"Sounds like a good idea." Ben ruffled his hair. "Well, come on down. Dinner's ready and Tess is waiting."

Jayden jumped off his bed and followed his father downstairs to the dining room.

MILES away in sunny Palm Beach, Florida, Kathryn hugged her knee-length cashmere sweater closer to her body and made herself more comfortable on her daybed. She stared at the Facebook message screen on the notebook computer, tapping the keyboard impatiently as she waited for Jayden to respond. After a few minutes of waiting, she typed: *'Are you still there?'*

Again receiving no response, she closed out of the screen and looked at the wall clock. It was easy to forget they were in different time zones. While it was early morning in Florida, it was night-time in New Farm, Queensland. Either Ben or his new wife must have made Jayden go to bed. She didn't know whether to be happy or sad about Ben remarrying. She couldn't be angry. After all, she'd been the one to leave him for Luke Emerson.

Luke. The wealthy play boy golf legend who'd left her starstruck after their initial meeting, sweeping her off her feet and into a new, glamorous lifestyle she thought would only come true in her wildest dreams. He'd showered her with affection and attention and made her feel more special than she'd ever felt in all the years she'd been married to Ben. But that affection had been waning of late. Luke was playing a golf tournament in Ireland and she hadn't been invited. Sure, they'd had their little spats before, but this was the first time he'd left to play without taking her to watch him and to be by his side for the media photo ops afterwards.

She sighed and rested her cheek in her palm as she stared out of the floor to ceiling windows looking out onto the magnificent Mediterranean estate. When she'd first seen it, the size of the grounds and the grand opulence had blown her mind. When they moved in, Luke laughed with her as they ran around like children exploring the estate. Not a very grown up or mature thing to do, but they didn't care. The lake sitting between the front entrance and the house gave only a hint of what was to come. In the back their private beach beckoned them. *A private beach! How many people have one of those?* Italian style Loggias framed a courtyard containing fountains, two pools and a Spanish garden. A seven-car garage topped it off. And that was just the outside.

She suddenly grew morose. How she wished she could wind the clock back. She wanted to be close to Luke again. To have him hold and kiss her like he used to. To look at her with nothing but love in his eyes.

A maid called her name and she snapped out of her reverie, turning away from the sunlit window. One of the five Spanish maids stood in the doorway with tea, a sponge cake and the morning paper. "Thank you, Camila." Kathryn took the acacia wood tray. "Just what I need."

"You're welcome." Camila's soft, caring voice always amazed her. "Are you all right, Ma'am? You don't look your normal self."

"I didn't sleep very well last night, so I guess I'm just a little tired."

Camila smiled warmly and nodded. "Well, if that's all, I'll leave you now, but let me know if there's anything else I can get for you. And perhaps you should take a nap later."

"I think I will, thank you." Kathryn appreciated the consideration the maids showed her even though she was only Luke's girlfriend and not his wife. She often wondered what it was like to live one's whole adult life as a servant to someone else. She couldn't imagine herself as a maid. After one week she'd become bored with the work and want to move on to more exciting things. Like lazy luncheons with other high society women that often stretched into the evening.

She took a sip of the hot orange spiced tea and lapsed back into thinking of Luke. Lately, she'd been pressuring him to marry her, but he always responded with the same lame excuse, *"I'm not ready to settle down, Kathryn."* Maybe that was why he hadn't taken her with him to Ireland. He didn't want her pestering him about marriage when he had an important game to play. She sighed, a heavy weight sitting in her chest as she bit into the sponge cake. *If he's not ready now, will he ever be?*

Opening the thick newspaper, she flipped to the sports

section. She scanned through the soccer scores, but stopped to look through the golf stories in full. There was a feature about Luke. She gasped and nearly dropped her tea cup as she stared at the picture of him and a blonde bombshell hanging on his arm as they left some sort of club. The photo was slightly blurred, like many she'd been captured in as the paparazzi snapped away at them whenever they were out in public. Despite the blurriness, Luke's features were unmistakable.

Kathryn's eyes watered as she swallowed the lump in her throat. *This can't be happening.* She squeezed her eyes shut and pressed a shaking hand to her forehead. When she opened her eyes, the photo still stared back at her. She put her tea cup down, snatched up the paper, and flung it across the room, her heart racing with anger.

She jumped to her feet and began pacing. This couldn't be happening. She was Luke's one true love. How many times had he told her that? A whole range of possible scenarios ran through her mind, but as she thought about and rejected each one, there was only one explanation left.

Luke had cheated on her.

Her skin tingled and she felt winded, as if a golf ball had hit her in the stomach. She sank to the couch as gut wrenching sobs rose from deep within. How could Luke have done this to her? He'd told her he loved her. She sobbed until she could sob no more, and her anger gave way to a deep sadness that sat heavily in her heart.

She slowly sat and wiped her face before reaching for the gold inlaid cigarette case Luke had given to her early in their relationship. Her hands shook as she took out a cigarette and lit it. As she drew long and deep, her hands steadied, but her heart was broken and she knew it would never recover.

She would confront Luke. As soon as that double-crossing piece of filth returned, she'd be waiting. And he'd pay. Oh yes, he'd pay.

CHAPTER 19

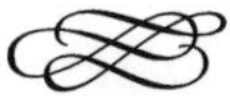

Tessa woke to the alarm as the first rays of sun poked through the small gap between the curtains. She rolled over and placed her arm gently on Ben's chest. "Are you ready for this, my sweet?" She reached her hand up and slowly turned his face to hers.

"Do we have to go?" His eyes were still closed, and his voice trailed off as he slipped back into sleep.

"Poor baby. Yes, we do. We promised Jayden." She leaned forward and kissed his cheek before jumping out of bed. Her stomach convulsed and she raced for the bathroom, just making it. When she returned a few minutes later, Ben had rolled over and was snoring. She let out a soft sigh and was tempted to climb back in with him, but she couldn't. They'd promised Jayden, and a deal was a deal. She'd leave him for a few minutes while she showered and dressed. Jayden wasn't up yet anyway.

As the hot water splashed over her body, her thoughts

turned to the camping trip. The week had been so busy they'd packed the car only the night before. Ben had been so particular about how to pack everything, they'd almost had a full on argument. It had taken all of her patience to let him do it his way, but it took forever. They would definitely need a bigger car when the baby was born.

At least the day was sunny. How would Ben have coped if it had been raining? He hated dirty shoes; what would he do with muddy ones? She let out a small giggle as the warm water flowed over her body. She so hoped the camping trip would be a fun time for them all. *"Oh Lord, please let us have a great time. Let it be full of fun and fellowship, and Lord, please help Ben cope with everything. And please keep working on Jayden. Thank You that he's continued coming to church, now I pray he'll see the magnificence of Your creation and will reach out to You as a result. Thank You for my family, God, and for this new little baby. Please bless us all, in Jesus' name, Amen."*

When she stepped out of the shower, the alarm was bleating and Ben was reaching out to turn it off. Yawning and stretching, he pulled himself upright and leaned against his pillows.

"Hey there, sleepyhead. Time to rise and shine." Tessa slipped on a comfy pink T-shirt and her new denim shorts with the elastic at the back and threw open the curtains.

Ben covered his eyes against the bright sunlight. "Guess I don't have a choice?" He peered at her between his fingers and raised an eyebrow. The corners of his mouth lifted slowly into a mischievous grin.

Tessa laughed and hit him playfully with a pillow before falling into his arms. Propping herself on her elbows, she tapped him on the lips. "No, you don't. We told Neil we'd pick him up at eight, so you'd better get moving." She leaned forward and planted a quick kiss on his lips before jumping up and running down the stairs to pack the last minute things.

The drive up to the rain forest hinterland took several hours. Jayden and Neil sat with headphones on listening to music most of the way and Ben and Tessa chatted about things in general. Neither had been to the hinterland for many years, and never together, so they enjoyed the changing scenery and just being out together, away from the everyday hustle and bustle of living and working.

Expansive acreage lots with horse paddocks and hobby farms soon gave way to sub-tropical foliage and winding roads snaking up the mountains to where it was cool and lush. The camp ground they'd chosen was surrounded by towering ghost gums and tree ferns, and was only a short walk from a large waterhole where the sounds of children jumping and splashing greeted them as they piled out of the car.

Tessa stretched as she gazed around and breathed in the cool, crisp mountain air. Someone's campfire still smouldered, sending a thin spiral of smoke across the campsite dotted with a range of tents in all different shapes and sizes. A spot on the edge of the clearing caught her eye. It was perfect. A small fireplace sat to one side of a flat area just big enough for their two small tents. They could lie in their sleeping bags and look out into the forest in the morning. What better way to wake up?

Ben had walked with the two boys to find the toilet and they were on their way back. Her heart fell as she saw the unimpressed look on his face.

"You didn't tell me they'd be drop toilets. They're the most disgusting things I've ever seen."

"Yeah, they smell gross." Jayden held his nose and made a face.

Tessa shook her head and laughed. "You boys! What do you expect up here in the mountains? Flushing toilets with full facilities?"

"That would be nice." Ben was serious.

She hit him playfully on the back. "Don't let a silly toilet ruin our weekend. Come on, let's set up." She headed to the back of the car and went to open the boot, but was surprised when Ben offered to do it.

"Boys, come and set up your tent." He threw them the small bag holding Tessa's old tent, while he carried the larger bag to the cleared area. Jayden and Neil opened their bag while she helped Ben.

"Yew!" Jayden threw the tent on the ground and jumped back.

The tent, covered in powdery mildew, disintegrated before her eyes. Her jaw dropped, and she slapped her hand over her mouth. How could this have happened? Last time she and Stephanie used it, it was fine. *But the weather wasn't...* It had rained and she'd meant to put it out to dry. Her shoulders fell. *I should have listened to Dad and checked it.*

"Now what are we going to do?" Jayden flung his arms out and stared at her with accusing eyes.

"Yes, Tessa. What are we going to do?" Ben's eyebrows arched as he stood there gazing at her with an amused expression on his face.

She drew a deep breath as she quickly thought of options.

"Jayden, Neil, I'm sorry. I should have checked the tent. We'll think of something, even if we have to drive to town and buy a new one."

"We could just sleep out, Mrs. Williams. I've done it before." Neil's face lit up. "Sleeping out's cool."

"It'll be cool all right. You'll freeze." Ben shook his head and stood with his arms crossed.

Tessa placed her hand on her hip. She wasn't going to let this ruin their weekend. "No, I think it could work. We could put the tarpaulin over them. I think they'd be fine. It's not like it's mid-winter." She slipped her arm around his waist, tilting her face towards his, hoping to convince him. "Come on, Ben. Relax. Everything doesn't have to be perfect to have a good time. It'll be an adventure for the boys to sleep out."

His eyebrows came together. "You really think they'll be okay? What if something happens to them?"

"Like what?

"Oh, I don't know. They could get bitten by a snake."

"Snakes don't normally come out at night."

"A spider, then."

"They've got their stretchers, so they'll be off the ground. They'll be fine. Loosen up a bit, hey?"

"You should have checked the tent."

"I know, and I'm sorry." Leaning up, she pulled his head down and kissed him. "Come on, let's get it sorted."

She breathed a sigh of relief as the two boys busied themselves setting up their outdoor sleeping area. Before long, hers and Ben's tent was up, and Jayden and Neil had finished their makeshift arrangement and were keen to find the waterhole.

"Why don't you go with them, Ben? I'll finish off here and

then come down." Tessa glanced up from sorting the basic cooking equipment as he packed the empty bags back into the car.

He closed the boot and walked over to join her. Slipping his hands around her waist, he nuzzled her neck, bringing goose bumps to her skin. "I can wait. Besides, I don't think I'm in to jumping off cliffs."

"Go on, you'll have fun. It'll do you good to spend time with the boys." She turned and grabbed his shirt with both hands, gently pulling him towards her. She leaned up and planted a kiss on his lips. "I'll come down soon."

His eyes twinkled. "I'd rather stay here with you."

"Ben!" Her eyes widened and she glanced sideways to where Jayden and Neil were standing and snickering.

Ben chuckled. "All right. I'll go." He held her gaze before lowering his head and kissing her more passionately than she thought he should with the boys watching. "But I'd rather be here," he whispered into her ear.

She slapped him playfully and pushed him away. *If only it was just the two of them...*

LEFT BY HERSELF, Tessa sat on one of the folding camp chairs and smiled to herself at Ben's unexpected display of affection. She'd been wondering if he'd be game to make love to her in a tent. After that kiss, she had no doubt whatsoever. Ever since she'd told him she wasn't seeing Michael, he'd been so much more at ease, and it warmed her heart.

She breathed in the fresh air as she finished the coffee

brought from home, and flicked through a magazine before wandering down to find the boys.

They weren't hard to find. She followed the yelling and yahooing and soon found the waterhole where a dozen or so children and teenagers, and a few adults, were climbing along a rock wall and leaping off into the water twenty or so metres below. As they clambered back up the rock face to do it all over again, some were blue in the face and others held their arms around their bodies and shivered, but all seemed keen despite the freezing water.

Apart from Ben.

Tessa laughed. Ben sat, arms wrapped around his knees on a flat rock in the sun, with his shirt still on. Jayden stood on the opposite side with Neil beside him, both ready to jump.

"Hey, Dad! Watch this!" Jayden leaped into the air, pulling his knees up and wrapping his arms around them, before landing heavily and making a large splash in the water. He bobbed up out of the water with a huge grin on his face.

"Come on. It's great." He couldn't wait to get back up there.

Tessa sat beside Ben and slipped her arm through his. "Go on. Go with him." She squeezed his hand and if she could, she would have forced him up.

His shoulders slumped. "This isn't me. I don't go jumping off cliff faces into the unknown."

"I know you don't. But do it for Jayden." She squeezed his hand again, and when he dragged himself up, gave him a smile brimming with encouragement.

She gazed lovingly at him as he clambered along the rocks, following Jayden and Neil, who both kept looking back to make sure he was still coming. She couldn't wait to see him leap off into the air.

Michael would have had a ball. In fact, he would have jumped and dive-bombed all day if he could. Tessa's heart grew heavy. She shouldn't have thought about Michael. No doubt he would have read her email by now, but he hadn't replied, not that she expected one. He would most likely be in Brisbane right now, staying with Sabrina. *I hope he had words with her...* Funny she hadn't seen Sabrina since that night in the car park. Seemed like Sabrina was avoiding her.

Jayden yelled and waved to her across the waterhole, drawing her away from her thoughts. She waved back. It was so good to see him behaving like a normal kid. Ben stood beside him, the rigid set of his jaw made her laugh again. Poor Ben. He'd much rather play chess than jump off a cliff. He'd told her that as an only child of well-to-do parents, he'd not only never been camping, he'd rarely done anything risky. The most challenging thing he'd ever done was abseil down a wall inside a gymnasium. He'd have to steel himself big time to leap into the unknown.

Neil jumped first. Jayden was left to coax his dad. Clever boy. If he'd jumped and left Ben on his own, Ben would never do it. But would he? *Could he?* The longer he waited, the harder it'd be. *Come on, Ben, just do it.*

He inched forward. No doubt he would have calculated how far down it was, how far out he'd need to jump, and how deep in the water he'd go. He would also have calculated the displacement of the water, but he wouldn't know the pain he'd feel if he landed badly. *You can do it!*

She would love to have done it with him, but Ben would never have approved, given 'her condition'.

He stood as still as one of the guards in front of Buckingham Palace, poised and steeling himself. Jayden, crouched beside him, continued to coax. Tessa's heart was in her mouth and her fingernails dug into the palms of her hands. As Ben finally jumped, she held her breath.

Moments later he hit the water and disappeared.

CHAPTER 20

Tessa leapt to her feet. Ben should have surfaced. Her hand flew to her chest. Her heart raced. *Where is he?* Everyone else who jumped bobbed up within seconds. Why hadn't he? Jayden's face paled as he stared into the water. Surely nothing could have happened to him? He'd jumped well clear of the rocks, and countless others had landed exactly where he had. Maybe he'd stopped breathing when he hit the freezing water. A thousand thoughts bombarded Tessa's mind.

Just as she moved closer to the edge, Ben broke the surface, one arm thrust into the air and a huge grin on his face. Tessa let out the breath she didn't know she'd been holding. The hide of him! But he'd done it, he'd survived it, and he'd enjoyed it. She relaxed.

Ben went round again several times while she watched on with pride, the obvious enjoyment on his face warming her heart.

. . .

LATER THAT NIGHT after they'd had dinner, they took a short walk to a clearing where the night sky was clearly visible. Lying on their backs, they gazed up at the myriad of stars twinkling down on them. Tessa rested her head on Ben's shoulder and sighed contentedly.

They remained silent as they gazed at God's handiwork. Beside them, Jayden and Neil tried to pick out constellations.

"I'm glad you made me come. It's been a good day." Ben kissed the side of her head and pulled her close.

"Yes, it has. And the boys have had a great time." She turned her head. "I'm sorry about the tent."

"Seems it's not a problem for them, so I guess it's not a problem at all."

"That's a first, Mr. Williams!"

"There have been a few firsts today, Mrs. Williams."

"And I think there'll be another tonight." She chuckled as she cuddled him playfully.

Ben leaned closer to her and whispered in her ear, "Yes, and I'm looking forward to it."

She giggled. "You're naughty."

"No I'm not." He let out a small laugh. "Now, let's sort out these stars."

TESSA WOKE WITH A START. Was that thunder? She lay rigid on her air mattress, not game to move lest she wake Ben, straining to hear the noise again. A faint rumble in the distance. She clenched her hands together as her heart beat faster. Storms hadn't been forecast when she'd checked a few days ago. If one hit it'd be disastrous, especially with the boys in their makeshift tent. For what seemed ages, she lay still, hoping and praying the storm wouldn't eventuate. But the rumble became closer and louder, until a clap, almost directly overhead, made her jump. Her hand flew to her chest as another clap of thunder boomed above.

Ben jerked upright. Lightning split the sky, illuminating the inside of the tent. His eyes were wide open. "Was that thunder?"

She grimaced. "Sounds like it, but storms weren't forecast."

The zip on the tent ripped open and the two boys piled in. "We're not staying out in that!" Jayden sat huddled with his sleeping bag around his shoulders. "It's monstrous!"

"It can't be that bad." Ben tousled Jayden's hair.

"You weren't out there. Go see for yourself."

Ben peeked out as a bolt of lightning cracked through the sky, with a loud clap of thunder following almost immediately.

"You're right. It's huge. And here comes the rain." He zipped up the tent and huddled close to Tessa.

"And the wind." She waited with baited breath, her arms clasped tightly around her knees. Within seconds, the wind hit, pushing the side wall of the tent in so much she and Ben had to bend their heads to avoid touching the sides.

"How long is it going to last?" Jayden yelled.

"Hopefully not long," she yelled back.

The tent wall was pushed in even further. "I think it's going to collapse." Ben tilted his head to look at the angle of the wall.

"No, it'll hold," she assured him. "Just sit tight." But her heart was pounding. The tent could cave in, but she didn't want to alarm Ben any further.

A crash outside made them all jump. "It's just the billy," she said, hoping she was right.

"How are we going to sleep?" Jayden asked.

"We won't until it passes," Neil replied.

"Maybe we should pray." Ben was almost hyperventilating.

"It's not that bad. We're not going to die!" Tessa let out a small laugh as she cuddled him. "But yes, maybe we could pray anyway. It won't hurt."

"You start." Ben's breathing began to steady.

"Okay, let's pray. But let's hold hands while we do."

"Do we have to?" The tone of Jayden's voice left no room for misunderstanding how he felt.

"Yes, we do." Ben's voice had firmed, and Tessa smiled quietly to herself as she squeezed his hand and at the same time took Jayden's.

"Dear Heavenly Father, thank You that You're with us now, right in the midst of this storm. I'm sorry I'm shouting, Lord, but I'm not shouting at You. Promise. Lord, please still our hearts, even though all around us is noise and chaos. We know that You're the Creator of all things, and this storm just shows us Your power and Your might. Your majesty is all around us, in the stars we gazed out at tonight, and in the beauty of this place. Be with us now we pray, and help us to trust You in the midst of all the storms we'll face in our lives, both now and in the future. Amen."

"Amen," Ben whispered as he returned her squeeze.

Jayden and Neil remained quiet and still as the storm slowly abated. Tessa's heart warmed as Jayden didn't flinch when she pulled him close. She prayed for him silently, asking God to touch his heart and to draw him slowly but surely into his Kingdom.

CHAPTER 21

Several weeks later on a Friday morning, Tessa woke earlier than usual. Something wasn't right, but she didn't know what. Her morning, or all day sickness, had decreased and she'd been feeling better of late, but this was different. Her stomach was cramping.

She said goodbye to Ben and Jayden and dragged herself to work, somehow making it through the day.

She almost didn't go to Bible Study, but decided the company of Christian women, especially Margaret, might help. *As long as Sabrina isn't there.* When she arrived a few minutes early and sat down beside Margaret, Margaret leaned over and patted her arm. "I've been praying for you, Tessa."

"Really? How thoughtful of you. Thank you." Tessa smiled and took a sip of her coffee before placing it on the table to the side. But she felt bad. She should have been praying for Margaret and Harrison more than the occasional times when she'd had a run in with Harrison. *If only I could be more like Margaret and learn to pray more.*

"Oh, it's nothing, really. Each week I choose a lady from our group to pray for. Last week it was Sally, and this week it's you." She turned, and facing Tessa square on, lowered her voice. "You were very much on my heart this week. As I was asking God what you needed prayer for, I believe He directed me to pray for extra strength for you."

Tessa's eyes welled. "Maybe it's because I've been feeling really tired." *How special to have someone care like this.*

Margaret searched Tessa's eyes with her own soft ones. "Apart from being tired, how have you been feeling of late?"

Tessa brushed her eyes and took a breath to steady herself. "I'm not getting sick anymore, but this morning I had the most painful of cramps. And two nights ago, I bled a little."

Margaret's eyes widened. "When was your last doctor's appointment?"

"Yesterday, the morning after I bled."

"What did he say?" She leaned closer.

Tessa sighed heavily. "He didn't seem very concerned. He checked me over and told me to come back in a few days for another check-up and a scan. I plan to go back tomorrow." As she placed her hands gently on her slightly rounded stomach, her chest tightened. "He said it wasn't anything to be worried about, but I can't help but be worried."

"I'm sure he knows what he's doing, but you have every right to be concerned, especially when you don't know what's happening."

Tessa bit her lip and forced her tears back. She didn't want to be the focus of attention, even amongst these caring women.

Margaret squeezed her hand, as if she knew exactly how she was feeling. "I'll be praying for you and your baby. Make sure you go back tomorrow and get checked out completely. You need to make sure your baby is okay."

Tessa nodded, sucking in a breath as she steadied herself. During their time of group prayer, she bowed her head and thanked God for bringing Margaret into her life. They'd become close, and Tessa appreciated the older woman's honesty and compassion. She would pray more often for her and Harrison, and she asked God if in some small way he might use her to help bridge the gap between the two.

She turned her attention to the group prayers. *"Lord God, we ask You to watch over Tessa and her baby, and to provide all they need in the days and weeks ahead. Pour Your blessings out on them both, and may Tessa and her husband know how deeply You care for them. Wrap Your loving arms around them now, Lord, and may their hearts be filled with Your peace. Amen."*

Tears flooded her eyes when Margaret prayed for her and her unborn baby. Margaret squeezed Tessa's hand again as Tessa wiped her tears away with the other. Margaret's prayer had touched her heart, although she didn't quite understand why. *I already know how much You care for me, God. I just need everything to be fine with my baby*. She caressed her tummy again and tried to focus on the study, but her mind and heart were elsewhere. She had a keen sense of God wrapping his arms around her, comforting her, but she didn't know why. Despite the chatter around her, she rested in His arms, and drew strength for whatever lay ahead.

. . .

IT WAS close to midnight when Tessa woke to searing pain in her stomach. Ben's arm was across her chest. The sheets, soaked with sweat, lay heavy on her body. She strained to sit upright but couldn't—the pain was too intense. "Ben." Her voice was weak and shallow. She nudged him gently with her elbow.

He stirred, but didn't fully awaken.

"I need to go to hospital." Her voice became more urgent as yet another wave of pain hit her.

Ben bolted upright in bed and leaned over her. "Hospital? What are you talking about?"

"The baby. I need to go now." She gripped her stomach as tears filled her eyes. She knew what was happening—she was miscarrying. She forced back a sob. *God, is this what You were preparing me for?*

"It's too early for the baby to be coming." Ben hurried out of bed, turned on the bedside lamp, and threw on a pair of jeans.

"I know." She grabbed his hand as fresh sobs collected in her throat.

EVERYTHING THAT HAPPENED NEXT WAS a blur. Ben knocked on Jayden's bedroom door and told him to get dressed. Then he was back in their bedroom, telling her she was going to be fine, wrapping her in a robe, and helping her out of bed. Every movement only increased the pain and Tessa bit her lip to keep from crying out loud. She was hardly aware of the ride to the hospital. Once there, a host of nurses and emergency workers surrounded her and placed her on a trolley bed as they rushed her inside. The bright lights of the hospital hallways swirled above her, the noise of the nurses talking sounded like yelling, and the beeping machines hooked up to her scared her. Tessa prayed for the tiny baby inside of her and fought to hold on to it. Her world was crashing down around her and she called out for Ben. Then the pain took over and she passed out.

SEVERAL LONG HOURS LATER, Tessa awoke. Her gaze moved around the room. Ben was sitting in a chair beside her bed, his head hanging low, holding her hand. Jayden was asleep in the only other chair in the room, wrapped in a dark green blanket. *Where am I, God? What's happening?* She eased herself slowly into an upright position as snippets of what happened flashed through her mind. The painful ride to the hospital, the bright lights, the noise, being wheeled away from Ben, *and our baby*. She slipped her hand out of his and clutched her stomach. *Empty*. Pain stabbed her heart as tears stung her eyes. She grabbed Ben's hand again. "Please tell me we haven't lost our baby." As she searched his face, she knew the answer. It was written all over it.

"We can try again." He kissed her forehead, her cheeks dampened with tears, her hands, her fingers, and drew her slowly into his arms. She sobbed uncontrollably into his chest. *God, why did You let this happen?* A dull ache grew inside her heart.

After some minutes, Ben lowered her back onto the pillows. She was numb and couldn't speak. He brushed her forehead with his hand and looked at her with such pity. She didn't want pity—she wanted her baby.

A soft knock sounded on the door before it was pushed

open and a red-headed nurse tip-toed in. "I'm sorry to interrupt." Her voice was courteous and quiet, like she really meant it. "The results are back from the internal, and I'm so sorry to confirm that you did miscarry." She paused, maybe to let the news sink in, but Tessa already knew. "This is a difficult moment for both of you, but it's not your fault, Mrs. Williams." She cast her gaze onto Tessa and stepped closer. "Miscarriage is very common—it's just not discussed a lot. But on the brighter side, the majority of women who miscarry go on to have a successful pregnancy next time round, so there's plenty of hope for the future."

The nurse meant well, but she was talking to someone else, not to Tessa. This wasn't happening. It hadn't happened. It was just a bad dream.

Ben thanked the nurse and she left the room.

"I'm sorry." Jayden's quiet voice sounded from the corner and made Tessa turn. His unexpected concern caused fresh sobs to catch in her throat. She forced them back and drew in a breath.

"Thank you. So are we." The thought suddenly hit her—Jayden was blaming himself for what had happened. She reached out her hand and when he took it, she drew him to her side and sat him on the bed.

"You're not to blame for this. No-one is." If only she could truly believe that for herself.

"But… I said I didn't want a brother or sister, and… and now I wish I could take back those words." His voice caught in his throat. He lifted his head and looked into Tessa's eyes. "I didn't mean them."

"I know you didn't." She wrapped her arms around him and let him sob into her chest.

Ben stood and placed his hand on Jayden's shoulder. "We've all had those heated moments when we say things we don't mean, son. Like Tessa said, it wasn't your fault, and with God's help, we'll pull through this."

After several long seconds, Jayden nodded and wiped his face with his sleeve. Ben didn't reprimand him.

"I think we should pray." Ben placed his other arm around Tessa's shoulders and led them in prayer, his words and his deep steady voice providing a degree of comfort. But they'd both been so convinced this baby was a gift from God, so why would He have let this happen? And how could Ben be so calm about it? He'd been over the moon about welcoming a new life into their family, and yet here he was, thanking God for His goodness. *It makes no sense, God. I don't understand.*

The swelling weight of disappointment and grief sat heavily on her heart, and she sobbed into Ben's arms. He pulled her close and kissed the top of her head as he stroked her hair. She knew deep down God would help them through this, but the ache in her heart hurt so badly, she could do nothing apart from cry for their lost baby.

CHAPTER 22

Tessa sat on the back porch swing holding a lukewarm mug of hot chocolate as she watched the sunset. The sky was a brilliant blaze of yellow, orange and red, but its beauty was lost on her. Her Bible lay open on the swing beside her, but every time she bent to read the words of Lamentations 3, tears filled her eyes. She was still trying to figure out why she and Ben had lost their baby. "What did we do wrong?" she asked God in between sobs. "What could I have done differently?" She sat silently, waiting for an answer, but none came.

She'd felt pain when she parted ways with Michael, but the pain she was experiencing now was like nothing she'd felt before. She was heartbroken, but also angry and worried. Angry that her body had failed her, and worried she might never carry a child to full term.

She leaned her head back and wiped away her tears with a crumpled tissue. She was tired of crying. She wanted to stop, but each time she thought her tears were all dried up, they'd start again with renewed fervour.

Her mother had assured her that despite the grief she was feeling right now, she would get over it. She herself had suffered a miscarriage in between Tessa and Elliott, and she knew what Tessa was going through. "Believe me, honey," her mother had assured her, "the pain will slowly decrease until one day you'll be able to think about the lost baby without crying."

Margaret had visited and given Tessa a list of Scripture passages she thought would be helpful and promised to keep praying for her. Fraser Stanthorpe and his wife, Tracey, had also visited. "No-one really knows why these things happen, but you shouldn't believe that your baby dying was God's doing." The pastor's eyes were full of compassion and understanding. "He's suffering with you, Tessa. He knows exactly how you feel, because he watched His own Son die in the most horrible of ways." He squeezed her hand. "Be comforted with the knowledge that your baby is now safe in His hands and one day you'll be reunited."

She was grateful for the outpouring of support and love she'd received from her friends and family, but she needed time to sort through her own thoughts. Ben and Jayden had left to pick up a few items she needed from the grocery store and had taken Sparky and Bindy for a walk at the same time. She closed her eyes. The doctor said the baby was a boy. She tried to picture what he would have looked like. What would she and Ben have named him? If he'd lived, how would he have changed their lives and who would he have become in the future? She'd never have the chance to know him or hold him in her arms, but a great love for the life she'd lost swelled within her. Fraser's words had comforted her to a degree. She liked the thought that their baby was in a better place, surrounded by angels, and being watched over by Christ Himself.

She dabbed her eyes and picked up the Bible laying open beside her. "I well remember them, and my soul is downcast within me. Yet this I call to mind and therefore I have hope," she read aloud. "Because of the Lord's great love we are not consumed, for His compassions never fail. They are new every morning; great is Your faithfulness."

Tears poured down her cheeks as warmth filled her heart. She drew in a long slow breath and bowed her head. "Oh God, I'm sorry. I'm sorry for not seeing the bigger picture but instead blaming both Yourself and me for the loss of our baby. I know You love me, even when I fail and when I ignore You. Thank You for Your great faithfulness and Your love. I will trust You to heal the pain in my heart, and to care for our dear little baby boy until we meet him face to face in heaven with You. In Jesus' precious name, Amen."

The faint ringing of the phone from inside the house interrupted Tessa's quiet time. She jumped up and ran inside, and picked up the phone just in time. Her heart skipped when she heard the familiar voice on the other end. "Stephanie! I'm so glad you called. I've been wanting to talk with you."

"No," the voice said. "This is Stephanie's mother, Vanessa."

"Oh, I'm sorry, Mrs. Trejo, you both sound so much alike. I still can't tell your voices apart after all these years." Tessa let out a small laugh but at the same time her chest tightened.

Why would Mrs. Trejo be calling? *Not more bad news, please, God. I can't handle it.*

"Stephanie's in the hospital. She was in a bad car accident last night."

Tessa's heart skipped a beat as she gripped the phone with both hands. "How… how bad is she?" Tessa could barely speak.

"She's not good." Mrs. Trejo's voice caught in her throat. "She's… she's got several broken bones, including a fracture in her spine." She broke down. "She might be paralysed for life." Tessa's heart began a freefall. *Stephanie, paralysed for life? This can't be happening.*

Tessa fell into the nearest chair as Ben and Jayden returned with the groceries. Ben dropped the bag he was carrying and rushed to her side. "What is it, Tess?" Ben's eyes had widened, and his voice was full of concern.

She lifted her watery eyes. Her heart felt like it was breaking. She sucked in a breath as she held the receiver to her chest. "Steph…" She took another breath and steadied herself. "Steph was in a car accident last night."

The colour drained from Ben's face. He sat down beside her and put his arm around her. Tessa lifted the receiver to her ear. Mrs. Trejo was still talking. "You girls have been friends for years, so I knew… I knew you'd want to know." Her voice had recovered a little but was still tight.

Tessa squeezed her eyes shut and steadied her breathing. "I'm so sorry, Mrs. Trejo. I…I don't know what to say, except that I'll be praying for you... for you both, and I'll come as soon as I can."

"I appreciate that, Tessa, I really do." She paused. "The police think it may have been deliberate."

Tessa sucked in a breath and straightened, her heart racing. "Deliberate? Why would they think that?"

Mrs. Trejo blew her nose. "It was a single vehicle accident. She wasn't under the influence of drugs or alcohol, and the weather was good. They think she drove her car off the road on purpose. But Stephanie would never do anything like that." Her voice strengthened. "I know my daughter. She just graduated, and she's got a great job, and—"

"She didn't tell you?" Tessa's voice came out soft and quiet.

Mrs. Trejo sucked in a breath. "Tell me what?"

Tessa let out a shaky sigh. "She lost her job a few weeks ago. She was really upset about it."

"No, I... I didn't know." She paused. "Maybe that's why she came to visit. I thought it odd, but she didn't say anything. I don't understand why she wouldn't have told me."

Tessa hurried to defend her friend. "I think she was afraid to disappoint you."

"Stephanie would never disappoint me." Mrs. Trejo's voice fell to a whisper. "I know I pushed her sometimes, but I could never be disappointed with her. Everything she did made me proud. I hope what you're saying isn't true, but if it is, I have only myself to blame. I hope I didn't push her too hard."

"I don't think you did, but she was very distraught over losing her job. I've never seen her so upset."

"My poor girl. If only she'd told me."

"She thought being at home with you would help. I'm sure she wouldn't have done this on purpose."

"I hope not too. Thanks for letting me know about her job. I'll let you know if anything changes. And please feel welcome to come whenever you can."

. . .

After hanging up, Tessa buried her face in Ben's chest and let him hold her. Neither spoke for some time. How could Stephanie be lying in a hospital bed, possibly paralysed for life? Harder even to process was the possibility Stephanie may have tried to take her own life, the last thing Tessa had imagined Stephanie would do. The scripture she'd read earlier came to her mind, and she clung to the promise that God's compassion would never fail, and that His faithfulness would see them through. Just right now, His faithfulness seemed to have eluded them.

CHAPTER 23

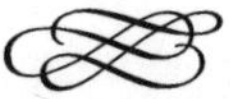

Before returning to the clinic, Tessa took a few days' leave to visit Stephanie. A change of scenery would do her good, plus she desperately wanted to see her friend.

Vanessa Trejo lived a three-hour drive north of Brisbane, on a hobby farm she and her husband had bought ten years earlier when they said they needed a 'tree change' from their overly busy city lives. Sadly, Roberto, Stephanie's father, passed away after only two years of moving there. Roberto might have avoided his massive heart attack if he'd sought medical advice earlier. After the funeral, Stephanie's mother decided to stay on and look after the farm on her own. "It's only ten acres after all," she'd said to the girls one weekend when they visited. Stephanie had encouraged her mother to return to the city, but Mrs. Trejo was determined to stay and run the farm on her own.

Now, as Tessa steered her car through the winding roads of

the lush, green Mary Valley, she considered the real benefits of living in a place as beautiful as this, away from the hustle and bustle of the city. A place where you could slow down a little. A place where kids could grow up enjoying the freedom of country living. A lump formed in her throat. Would she ever have children of her own? The loss of her baby was still so fresh and real, and the very thought of it brought tears to her eyes. "Oh God, please heal my hurting heart. And please be with Steph and her mum. I don't understand why all this has happened, but Lord I trust You to work it out. Thank You for this beautiful place. I pray that this time away will draw me closer to You."

The thought began to grow in her mind that maybe she and Ben and Jayden could move out here. She could easily get a job as a country vet, and it wasn't that far to the nearest town where Ben would no doubt find a job. But would Jayden like living in the country? Away from all his friends, especially Neil? She sighed. Probably not. *Maybe one day...*

Ten minutes later, Tessa pulled into the Trejo's farm. A sign reading *'Misty Morn'* hung on the wrought iron gates bordered on either side with rambling vines and overgrown bushes. Beyond the gates, a gravel driveway led to the cottage Stephanie's parents had just finished renovating before Mr. Trejo suddenly passed away. Mrs. Trejo loved flowering plants; the front porch was a mass of colour. Baskets overflowing with soft pink petunias, red geraniums and brilliant blue salvias lined the edge of the bull-nosed verandah, while soft pink azaleas and white daisies nodded in the garden below.

As she stepped out of the car and stretched, Tessa breathed in the fresh country air. Yes, she could live here.

Mrs. Trejo ran down the steps and gave Tessa a big hug. "Thank you for coming." She smiled at Tessa with moist eyes.

"Thank you for having me." Tessa smiled warmly at her friend's mother. They chatted easily about the garden and the farm as Mrs. Trejo showed Tessa to her room and put the kettle on. Not until they were sitting on the verandah with a cup of tea and freshly baked scones with jam and cream made from the milk of Mrs. Trejo's favourite cow, Mildred, did Tessa ask about Stephanie.

"How is she?" Tessa drew in a slow breath as she carefully placed her cup back onto its saucer and lifted her eyes to meet Mrs. Trejo's.

Her eyes moistened again. "She's on a lot of pain medication, and she's still in traction, but the doctors believe she won't walk again." She could hardly speak as tears flowed freely down her cheeks.

Tessa gripped her hand. Words weren't required.

Two hours later, Tessa entered Stephanie's hospital room. Stephanie's eyes were closed, so she sat quietly on the chair beside her. Mrs. Trejo was talking with the nurse. Tessa took Stephanie's hand and squeezed it. How had this happened? She inhaled slowly. "Steph, can you hear me?"

Stephanie's eyes blinked and slowly opened. "Tess…" Her voice was thin and raspy.

"Don't speak. It's all right."

She closed her eyes.

Tessa held her hand and gazed at her friend. Her heart was heavy, and she wondered what good could ever come of this.

She sighed deeply. *"God, I really don't understand why this has happened, but I have to trust that Your grace will be sufficient. Please be with Steph, and heal not only her body, but heal her spirit and mind as well. May she draw on Your strength at this difficult time, and know Your peace in her heart despite the pain in her body."*

Memories of another hospital bed came to Tessa's mind as she sat holding Stephanie's hand. Not that long ago she'd sat in a chair, not too dissimilar to the one she was sitting in now, holding Michael's hand and praying for his quick recovery. She didn't know why God hadn't answered her prayers at the time, but that didn't mean she couldn't trust God to answer her prayers now. God had still been working in Michael's life, even though it took longer than she'd hoped. She squeezed Stephanie's hand.

"God, I pray Stephanie handles this better than Michael did. Be her strength when she has none, give her hope when all seems hopeless, and every moment of every day, may she be aware of Your love for her. Bless my dear friend, Lord God, I ask in Jesus' name."

As she sat there, Tessa thought about the brief reply to her email Michael had sent. He'd congratulated her on her marriage and wished her well, but he hadn't mentioned how he was feeling. She wondered if she'd ever see him again, but somehow it didn't worry her anymore. She hoped he'd meet someone special, someone he could enjoy life with, grow old with. No doubt if she ever bumped into Sabrina again, she'd hear what he was doing.

. . .

Mrs. Trejo entered the room and took Stephanie's other hand. Stephanie's eyes fluttered and then remained opened for several seconds before closing again.

"This is what's she been like for days now." Mrs. Trejo's eyes held a deep sadness.

"She'll come round." Tessa tried to encourage her. "What did the nurse have to say?"

"They want to move her to a bigger hospital." Mrs. Trejo sighed wearily. "I'm not sure what's wrong with this one. They seem to have everything."

"I guess they just want to give her the best chance possible." Tessa let out a small sigh. If it were her, she'd be doing everything she possibly could for her daughter.

Mrs. Trejo nodded, but didn't look convinced.

"You're worried about how you'll manage, aren't you?"

She drew a breath. "It's difficult to leave the farm for more than a day at a time, but I want to be with Stephanie." She ran her hand over Stephanie's brow and gazed lovingly at her.

"I'm sure one of your neighbours could care for the animals if need be. It'll work out, you'll see. Try not worry about it."

She nodded again as tears welled in her eyes. Tessa couldn't start to imagine what she was feeling, seeing her only child lying in a hospital bed like this, and being told it was unlikely she'd ever walk again.

Tessa spent the next two days at the farm. They visited Stephanie twice a day and stayed with her for hours at a time. Stephanie slowly became more lucid, but whenever the pain became too much, she'd be given more drugs and she'd fall back into a deep sleep. Tessa hated seeing her like this, and was concerned about the amount of medication the doctors had prescribed.

Mrs. Trejo agreed to have her moved to the Spinal Unit at the Royal Brisbane Hospital, where she would receive expert care. The doctors were hopeful she might regain some movement in time. One of her neighbours agreed to care for her animals while she was with Stephanie, and she could stay with her sister in Brisbane as long as needed.

With Stephanie in Brisbane, Tessa could easily visit as often as she wanted, and on the drive home the following day, she felt more at peace than she had since losing the baby.

When she returned to the clinic after the week's absence, Tessa determined to be more positive about her role. Maybe God had put her here for a reason, and she should embrace the opportunity to grow and learn, and not run away from it.

Late that morning, a knock sounded on her office door and Harrison entered. "I don't mean to bother you." He stood awkwardly in front of her, and looked down at the ground. "I heard about your loss. I'm sorry."

Tessa's eyes widened. It was the last thing she expected him to say.

He lifted his gaze and looked uneasily at her. "I know I've caused you a few problems, but I actually think you're doing a good job running this place."

"Thank you. On both accounts." She gave him a warm smile. Was this an opportunity to speak to him about his mother? Her heart thumped at the thought of addressing the issue. *God, I've already prayed about this, so please give me the words to say.* She drew a slow breath.

Harrison turned to leave.

"Wait." She gulped.

He paused and turned to look at her.

"I've... I've been meaning to tell you this for some time." She paused. How would he take this? But it was no use worrying about it—she just needed to say it now the opportunity had arisen. She drew a steadying breath and went for it. "Your mother and I are good friends. We attend the same church and the same Bible study group." She held her breath.

Harrison stiffened. "You don't know anything about our relationship." His eyes narrowed.

"You're right, I don't. But she did tell me how saddened she is you haven't spoken in years."

"Did she put you up to this?" A vein in his neck bulged as he held her gaze.

"Not all." Tessa sighed. "It's just that my best friend was in a really bad car accident recently, and it reminded me of how short life is. You never know when you might lose a family member or friend."

Harrison turned to leave.

"Please listen to me. Your parents aren't going to be around forever. You might not have next year or even next week to get things right with them."

"I don't have anything to get right."

"Cutting them off, ignoring their phone calls, refusing to meet them, not sharing Christmas or birthdays..." She sucked in a breath and stopped herself. Had she said too much? Her voice softened. "Don't you see anything wrong with that?"

A moment of silence passed between them before Harrison gave a careless shrug. "I'll give it some thought."

"Please do. For both your sakes."

He pursed his lips and without saying another word, spun on his heels and left her office.

CHAPTER 24

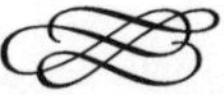

That evening, Jayden walked into the living room, head down and shoulders slumped. Tessa knew it was necessary, but she hated the times when Ben called a sit-down meeting with Jayden to discuss his falling grades and less than acceptable behaviour and attitude. She sat on the edge of the sofa beside Ben, clasping her hands over her knees.

Jayden slouched in a seat opposite, arms folded and glaring at his dad. "What have I done wrong now?"

Ben held up Jayden's latest school report. "One B, two Cs, and the rest are Ds. How do you explain that?" Ben's tone was measured and controlled, but could easily escalate at any moment.

Jayden stared straight ahead, his eyes vacant. His foot bounced restlessly as if he'd rather be anywhere else other than here. He didn't respond.

"I'm still waiting for an answer." Ben leaned forward.

Jayden lowered his gaze until the hair hanging over his

forehead covered his eyes. He shrugged carelessly. "I'm doing my best."

"You can't be. You've always been a straight A student." Ben let out an exasperated sigh. "I've a fair mind to ground you until you improve."

Tessa's heart fell. *Here we go again.* She touched Ben's arm lightly.

Ben's jaw clenched as he glanced at her briefly before returning his attention to Jayden. "Have you got anything to say for yourself? Look at me."

Jayden lifted his head slowly but only met his father's gaze for a second before fixing it on the coffee table.

Tessa sighed quietly. Her heart was breaking for Jayden. If only Ben would show more compassion. There'd been odd moments when they'd gotten on better, but not nearly enough, and it grieved her no end. *Lord, please intervene in this situation. Please help Ben and Jayden talk with each other in a reasonable manner, without all this angst that's not doing anyone any good.*

A minute passed, then two. Tension filled the air.

Jayden finally lifted his gaze. His eyes had watered. "There is something, but it's not to do with my grades. If I tell you, will you be angry?"

Tessa held her breath.

Ben pursed his lips. "Depends what it is."

She grabbed his hand and gave him an angry stare. Her heart rate increased. Enough was enough. She wasn't going to let him ruin this opportunity. She shifted her gaze to Jayden and leaned forward. "We won't be angry, Jayden. Whatever you tell us, we're a family, and we'll find a way through it. Won't we, Ben?" The glance she gave him left no room for him to disagree.

Jayden's gaze flickered between the two of them. Tessa didn't dare look at Ben again, but she could feel the tension in his body. More seconds passed.

Ben blew out a long breath. "Yes, Tessa's right." His voice had softened. "We're a family, and we'll work through it together. Whatever it is."

Jayden wiped his eyes with the back of his hand. "I've been dumped from the Rubgy team. I won't be playing any more this season."

"Oh Jayden. I'm so sorry." Tessa moved to the couch beside him and placed her arm around his shoulder. "It's not the end of the world. It's okay."

He blinked and sat still, his head hanging.

Ben rubbed his temple. "I'm sorry, but I'm not surprised after seeing your game the other week." His forehead puckered. "But I don't understand why you're suddenly failing at everything. First your grades, and now your sport." He paused, settling his gaze on Jayden. "What's next?"

"I knew you'd be angry." Tears ran down Jayden's cheeks as he pushed Tessa's arm away and jumped up. "It's obvious I can't do anything right." He knocked a chair over and ran upstairs to his room.

Ben ran after him. "I didn't mean it like that." The door slammed in his face.

Tessa had followed Ben up the stairs and grabbed his hand. "Leave him,." Her heart thumped. "Let him cool down for a while."

Ben turned around and ran his hands through his hair.

Tessa's heart went out to him. He looked so distraught. She held her arms out and stepped closer, drawing him close.

He leaned his head on hers. "I always get it wrong. I'm no good at this." His voice was broken.

"It's okay. He'll calm down and then we can talk again. Let's go back downstairs." She took his hand.

He let out a deep breath as he followed her down. "What if he's on drugs or something like that?" He paused mid-stair. "What else would have caused such a big change?"

Tessa turned to face him. "I don't know, but we can try to find out. His teachers might have some insight when you meet with them next week."

"You're right. We need to get to the bottom of it. Something's happened, and I don't like it."

When they reached the kitchen, Tessa filled the kettle and turned it on. "By the way, did you know Jayden doesn't love rugby as much as rowing or tennis?"

Ben angled his head. "What do you mean? He's never said anything to me about that."

"He told me when we were at the dog park a while ago. He was playing because he thought you'd be disappointed if he didn't." She took two mugs out of the drawer and chuckled. They weren't in orderly rows anymore.

"He should have told me he didn't want to play." Ben raked his hand through his hair. "I'll go and talk with him about it."

Tessa lifted her eyes and met his gaze. "Not yet. It might be best to let him cool off some more first." She placed a teabag into each mug and filled them with boiling water before carrying them to the sofa.

Ben took a mug from her. "I'm sorry for getting angry. I just don't know what to do with him."

The drawn expression on his face concerned her, and she leaned in to him and squeezed his hand. "He'll be fine. He's just going through a rough patch at the moment. I'm sure he'll come through it."

Ben rubbed the back of his neck. "I hope you're right." He kissed the top of her head. "Maybe we should take a holiday and get away from everything for a while."

Tessa's eyes lit up as she straightened. "That's a great idea. Let's do it!"

After a few days of discussion, they made the decision to take two weeks off over the next school break and go skiing in Queenstown, New Zealand. Tessa had always wanted to learn how to ski and Ben had always wanted to visit Queenstown, so it was a win-win for them both. Jayden also brightened when he was told about the trip. He brightened even further when he was allowed to invite Neil as well—a kind of birthday present since he'd be celebrating his fifteenth birthday just before they left. He promised to try harder at school, and apologised for letting his grades go. His teachers had also been concerned about his falling grades, but had no explanation for the sudden change. Tessa convinced Ben to lay off him a while.

Time flew, and before they knew it, they were lining up at the check-in counter for their eagerly anticipated holiday. Tessa had left the clinic in Harrison's care, a decision she'd made on the spur of the moment, but somehow it had felt right, and Bindy and Sparky were staying with her parents.

Her phone rang as they sat in the boarding lounge. Ben had just handed her a coffee, so she took a sip before answering. It was Margaret, and she was so emotional, Tessa could hardly understand her.

"Tessa, you... you aren't going to believe this." Her voice caught in her throat. "I can hardly believe it myself."

"Margaret, what's happened?" Tessa's heart pounded. Could it be? Could it really be that Harrison had finally contacted his mother? What else would make her so emotional? Tessa could think of nothing else that would touch her friend so deeply. She hoped that it truly was the breakthrough they'd both been praying for.

Margaret sucked in a breath and continued. "Harrison called this morning." She began to sob.

Tessa's eyes blurred with tears. "That is such great news! I'm so happy for you."

Margaret sniffed. Gradually her sobs subsided, allowing her to continue. "Thank you. I'm so happy, I hardly know what to do with myself." Her voice held such excitement that Tessa imagined her jigging on the spot like a teabag, and it made her smile.

"God really is good, isn't He?" Tessa let out a contented sigh.

"He is. I'd almost given up hope." Margaret took a deep breath. "It was wrong of me, I know, but it's been so long." She paused, sniffing once again. "I somehow have a feeling He might have used you in some way, so thank you. I'm so glad we became friends."

"Me too, Margaret. Me too."

A short while later, as they all settled into their seats for the three and a half hour flight to Queenstown, Tessa couldn't help but think that things were finally starting to look up.

CHAPTER 25

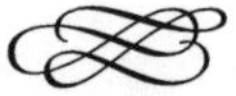

Standing atop the north-facing slopes of The Remarkables ski area, Tessa's gaze swept across Lake Wakatipu and the surrounding alpine resort of Queenstown and her jaw dropped. "I knew it would be amazing, but it's… it's breathtaking." Sun-kissed alps pierced the whiter than white clouds hovering over the peaks, and stood in stark contrast with the brilliant blue sky stretching as far as the eye could see.

She shivered slightly as the fresh mountain air lightly brushed her face. Shifting unsteadily on her skis, she turned to the three males standing beside her and couldn't help but grin. Jayden and Neil, so cool in their ski outfits, were eager to tackle the slopes. Ben's day-old stubble gave him a slightly rugged appearance, and she loved the way his designer ski clothes hugged his tall, lean body.

A male instructor slid to a stop in front of them, sending a spray of powdery snow into the air. He dug his poles into the snow and removed his goggles. An easy grin sat on his deeply sun-tanned face. A neatly trimmed moustache gave him a slightly European look, and his crystal-blue eyes sparkled.

"Pretty cool, huh? I've been skiing these slopes since I was a kid, but I don't think I'll ever tire of their beauty." He pulled off his gloves and extended his hand first to Ben and then to Tessa and lastly to the two boys. "Eversley Scalet. Nice to meet you all. Is this your first time?"

Ben replied first. "I've skied before, but a long time ago."

"This will be our first time." Tessa stretched her arm behind the two boys, drawing them closer.

"No problem." Eversley smiled easily. "The Remarkables are perfect for beginners and pros alike. You boys ever been snow-boarding?"

"No," Jayden replied.

"But we can skateboard, if that helps any," Neil added.

"Not exactly." Eversley laughed. "Skateboarding and snow-boarding do have some similarities, but they're completely different sports. I'm going out to the back country this after-noon to do some snowboarding. If you're interested, I'd be happy to teach you some moves."

"That would be cool," Neil said. "We'd love to come."

"Great, but first things first," Eversley said. "I suggest we start on the learners' slopes instead of up here." He raised his ski pole and pointed away to a set of lower mountains. "A chairlift will take us over there. Beginner runs aren't as steep, so you won't run into as many obstacles and hopefully you'll also take fewer tumbles."

"Tumbles?" Tessa's jaw dropped. "I'm petrified of falling

down a precipice." She grimaced as she glanced over the side of the mountain that disappeared into oblivion.

Eversley chuckled. "Don't worry, I'll show you how to fall so you don't hurt yourself. You'll be right if you stay away from the edges and take it easy." He grinned, revealing a row of even, white teeth. "The most important thing after you take a tumble is to get back up and try again... and again and again."

Tessa gave him a half-hearted smile. She didn't know why she was so nervous, after all, she could ride a bicycle; she loved snorkelling and hiking and most other sports, but there was something about the slippery snow and the long pointy skis that made her unsteady on her feet.

Despite her initial concerns, all morning long, the four of them practiced skiing down the beginner slopes under Eversley's expert instruction. True to his word, they took a lot of tumbles, but not even Tessa minded too much. Their time was full of fun and laughter. It felt so good to be out of New Farm and away from the everyday pressures of work and school. There was a certain spirit of freedom on the mountains and she and Ben especially relished it.

When their lesson was over, they thanked Eversley and headed back to The Remarkable Mountain Lodge where they were staying.

After changing clothes, warming up, and eating lunch, she and Ben settled into the lodge's movie room with two steaming cups of hot chocolate topped with puffy marshmallows.

"Would you like to join us?" she asked Jayden and Neil.

"Maybe another time," Neil replied, tucking the striped blue and white board he was holding more securely under his arm.

"We're off to do some snowboarding with Eversley." He nudged Jayden who was blocking the doorway, engrossed in his phone.

"What?" Jayden snapped.

Neil took a step back and stared at him. "Did you forget? Snowboarding with Eversley? He's waiting outside for us now."

Jayden shrugged. "I'm not interested anymore. You can go by yourself."

Neil's eyes narrowed. "Oh, right, I forgot you're no longer interested in the things you used to be." His voice held a hint of sarcasm. "You're not interested in making music with our band anymore. You're not interested in playing rugby anymore. You're not interested in hanging around your own friend, who just happens to be me. And now you aren't even interested in learning how to snowboard."

"We don't have to hang around each other all the time to be friends." Jayden shifted his weight to his other foot. "Besides, I'm really not interested in any of those things anymore."

"Jayden, that's enough." Ben sprang out of his seat and stood over him. He was breathing heavily and the muscles in his neck tightened. "We didn't come all the way to Queenstown for you to stay stuck inside with your eyes glued to your phone screen. You'll go snowboarding with Neil and Eversley or I'll take your phone off you."

Tessa held her breath, her heart pounding. This wasn't meant to have happened.

Jayden rolled his eyes and slipped his phone into his pocket. "Whatever. These lessons better not take long. I've got other things to do."

Ben narrowed his eyes. "Like what, exactly?"

Jayden shrugged offhandedly as he turned to follow Neil. "Just stuff."

As soon as the boys were out of sight, Tessa pulled Ben back down beside her. His chest was still heaving and his body tense. She slipped her arm around his shoulder and snuggled close.

"Come on, relax. He went, that's the main thing." She leaned up and kissed him.

Ben let out a huge sigh and his body relaxed a little. "Yes, you're right." He kissed the top of her head. "I just don't know what to make of it. He annoys me so much sometimes."

"I know. He was super excited about being here in the beginning, so I don't know what's happened to make him so touchy now. Hopefully an hour or so with Eversley will help." She rested her head on Ben's chest and drew in a slow breath. She sincerely hoped that would be the case. They needed this holiday, and could do without hassles with Jayden.

Ben flicked on the screen and pulled her closer as he placed his feet on a footstool. "I hope you're right. I don't know how much patience I'll have if he stays like that for the rest of the holiday."

Tessa released a sigh and offered up a prayer.

EVERYONE AWOKE the next morning looking forward to another day filled with fun, snow, and sunshine—everyone except Jayden. He dragged around the slopes behind the other three and Eversley as if he didn't want to be there. He periodically stopped to check his phone.

When Eversley left to attend another group of skiers, Neil had an idea. "Let's have a race."

"Good suggestion," Ben agreed, placing his goggles over his eyes. "You should all be warned… I'm quite the competitor. Are you all ready?"

Tessa gave a mock haughty shake of her head. "Are you? Because I'm no pushover either." She strapped on her skis and hurried to get in position.

Neil waved for Jayden to get in line, but Jayden wasn't paying attention. His back was toward them and he was on his phone again. "Hey, Jayden, are you ready?"

"For what?" Jayden asked without turning around.

Neil frowned. He scooped up a handful of snow and packed it into a ball before flinging it at him. It splattered squarely into his back. "Will you put down that stupid phone and pay attention to what we're doing for a second? We're about to have a race."

Jayden spun around. "Did I say I wanted to race? No!"

"Boys, stop it!" Tessa intervened before Ben did.

Jayden ignored her and spoke to Neil. "Stop telling me what to do." He shoved his phone into his pocket, bent to scoop up a handful of snow, and threw it straight into Neil's face. Neil barely ducked in time. He recovered quickly, and rushed at Jayden.

"Enough," Ben shouted. Forgetting her skis were already strapped on, Tessa lurched forward to keep Jayden and Neil apart. As she tripped and fell, she tried to remember what Eversley told them about falling sideways instead of backwards or forwards, but it was too late. She crashed onto her back with her leg bent into an awkward position underneath her and began sliding down the slope.

She screamed and her heart skipped a beat as she plummeted further down the slope. *I'm going to die, I just know it...* Her heart pounded. She tried to grasp onto something to slow her slide, but she was moving too fast and all that surrounded her was snow. Dizzying whiteness blurred past, blinding her sight and stinging her skin as it scraped against the cold powder. She sucked in a breath, but snow slid down her throat almost choking her. Her body jolted as she came to a sudden halt.

Her head spun, and she could hardly open her eyes, but when she managed to open them, Eversley stood over her. It had been him she'd slammed into.

"Sorry." She could barely speak. She rolled over and tried to get up but winced at the pain in her foot. "I think I've broken something." Her voice was no more than a whisper.

Ben and Neil arrived. Ben stooped over her, his brows knitted. "Tessa, are you okay?"

She bit her lip as she tentatively reached for her ankle. "I hope so."

"Lay still and let me check," Eversley said. He bent down beside her and stretched out her legs. When he squeezed her left ankle, she stifled a scream.

"Seems it's just your ankle. I don't think it's broken, probably a bad sprain, but we'll get it checked out." He repositioned her foot carefully on the snow. "You're a lucky girl. It could have been a lot worse."

She groaned. This was bad enough.

"Can you walk?" Neil asked.

She shook her head. "I don't think so." She tried to get up but fell back into the snow.

"No walking," Ben said. "We'll carry you."

She looked up and caught his eye. He was so concerned about her, but she could kick herself. She'd ruined their holiday.

She winced as Eversley and Ben both put an arm around her and helped her take her weight on her one good foot before sitting her on their joined hands. She wrapped an arm around each of their shoulders and settled herself in her makeshift chair.

"Guess we'll have to race another time." Ben raised his brows and gave her a cheeky grin. He looked up suddenly. "Where's Jayden?" His eyebrows puckered as he scanned the area.

"I'll get him." Neil turned and jogged up the slope as best he could. After a few minutes, he came sliding back down, nearly barrelling into them. He stopped himself just in time.

"He's not there." Neil's face had lost all its colour.

CHAPTER 26

"You must be wrong. Jayden has to be somewhere." Ben scanned the area again as he desperately tried to remain calm.

Neil shook his head. "He's not where I left him, Mr. Williams, and I couldn't see him anywhere."

"He couldn't have just disappeared." Ben tried to remain calm, but his heart began racing dangerously fast as a whole range of possibilities ran through his head.

After leaving Tessa in the care of the medical staff, Ben returned to the slopes with Neil to thoroughly scour the area for Jayden. He'd called Jayden's phone countless times, but each time it just went straight to MessageBank. He couldn't understand it. Jayden always had his phone with him.

The weather had changed and dark clouds were rolling in, shrouding the peaks in masses of swirling grey. The beautiful mountains he and Tessa had been so in awe of just yesterday had morphed into foreboding monoliths.

"He must have fallen," Ben said to Neil for what seemed like the hundredth time. He couldn't voice the other thoughts crowding his mind. He swallowed hard as a chill ran through his body. *Surely Jayden hadn't been kidnapped.*

He looked hopeful as Eversley came towards him dragging an object behind him. "Anything?" Ben asked, trying not to sound over eager.

Eversley shook his head. Instead of his usual easy-going manner, his expression was grim. "No sign of him, but I found these."

Ben bit his lip to stop it trembling.

"They're Jayden's skis." Neil sounded alarmed. "He had them last time I saw him."

Ben's face paled. "I don't understand where he could have gone, and so fast. We were all here together when Tessa fell. I thought he'd followed us down."

"We'd better get a search party organised. And the quicker the better. I don't like the look of this weather." Eversley glanced up at the thickening clouds hovering overhead. "I think we're in for a blizzard."

Ben's heart fell. Where was Jayden? He drew in a deep breath as he gazed at the darkening clouds. *Please God, please don't let him be out in this on his own.*

As Ben followed Eversley back down the mountain slope to the lodge, his mind swarmed with questions he didn't have answers to. Jayden had either fallen, or he'd been kidnapped, but that was unlikely. More likely he'd walked off on his own accord given the mood he'd been in. But what had triggered it? Ben had no idea. And if he'd walked off, where would he have gone? *And why?* He couldn't have gone far. He couldn't drive, and he didn't have much money. *What if he'd met someone?* A heavy weight settled on Ben's chest. He'd heard of sick men stalking young boys. Surely Jayden was smarter than that. But he *had* been on his phone an awful lot. Who was he talking to?

Ben's heart rate increased the more he thought about it. All the things he'd confronted Jayden about—his grades, rugby, mixing with Owen, ran through his mind. They'd seemed important at the time, but paled into insignificance now Jayden was missing.

If he'd gone off willingly, Ben only had himself to blame. How many times had Tess told him to go easy on the boy? He hadn't listened to her, but now he wished he had.

Eversley contacted the manager, who quickly put an alert out to all instructors. He also contacted the Police and the Emergency Services. A missing fifteen-year-old boy out in this weather was a concern for everyone.

The Police interviewed Ben and Neil. They told the constable all they knew, which was very little. Tessa was wheeled in soon after and clung to Ben as best she could with her leg elevated in the wheelchair. One of the staff members gave them mugs of hot chocolate. Neil sat beside them quietly.

"I want to join the search team," Ben said to Eversley.

Eversley clapped him on the shoulder. "No, it's best you stay here. Keep your chin up. He couldn't have gone that far. I'm sure we'll find him."

Neil kicked his legs and fidgetted with his hands. "Do you think Jayden left because of me? Maybe I shouldn't have yelled at him and just left him alone. Seemed he didn't want to be bothered with me anyway."

Tessa wrapped her arm around him. "No, don't think like

that. It's not your fault. Like Eversley said, they'll find him, hopefully sooner rather than later. We don't know where Jayden is, but God does. We have to trust God in this situation, okay?"

Neil nodded, but didn't look convinced. He kicked his feet even more and then looked up. "I have something to tell you. I wasn't going to before, but I am now because it may help us find Jayden."

Ben straightened. "Go on. What is it?"

Neil blinked and paused before speaking. "Last week Jayden told me his mother contacted him." He glanced at Tessa. "His other mother."

"Kathryn?" Ben's eyes widened.

Neil nodded. "I don't know what they talked about exactly, but Jayden said he wanted to leave and live with her, so maybe that's what he did." Neil lowered his gaze.

Ben felt his face blanch. He shook his head. "No." He sunk back into the chair and held his head in his hands. "I don't believe it." His voice was barely a whisper.

Tessa gripped his leg.

Ben struggled to believe a word Neil had said. But if it was true, some of Jayden's strange behaviour would make sense. He'd always been on his phone or computer leading them to believe he was studying, when in reality it seemed now he was communicating with Kathryn.

He sucked in a deep breath and raised his head. "Why didn't you tell us this before?"

Neil looked up slowly and shrugged one shoulder defensively. "I didn't think he'd actually leave. I thought he was joking, but I guess I was wrong." Tears sprang to his eyes. "I'm sorry."

"You're not to blame for Jayden's actions," Tessa said quietly.

"What else did he say? Did he give any clue as to where he would have gone with her?" Ben leaned forward, his face almost touching Neil's.

"No, but I did think it was strange he was sorting his bag this morning."

"Let's look in your room." Ben jumped up, his heart pounding. How could Jayden have done this? To go off with Kathryn of all people.

Tessa grabbed his hand. "Shouldn't we tell the Police?"

He paused. As much as he wanted to go racing off and find any clue as to Jayden's whereabouts, maybe Tessa was right. He inhaled deeply and clenched his fists. "Yes, we should. Come on Neil, let's go." Ben placed his hand lightly on Neil's shoulder and directed him towards the Lodge meeting room where the Police and Emergency Services were co-ordinating their search.

Shortly after, they accompanied a constable into Neil and Jayden's room.

"Take a look and see if anything's missing first. Then we'll do a thorough search." The constable stood in the doorway while Neil rummaged through the small cupboard and the messy floor. Typical teenage boy's room. Clothes strewn everywhere, wet towels lying on top making everything else damp. Ben sighed. How many times had he told Jayden to clean his room up and not live like this? It didn't matter now.

"His small backpack is missing. And I think some of his

clothes. And his Mac." Neil's voice caught in his throat. "I'm sorry Mr. Williams. I should have told you what I knew earlier." He lowered his gaze and brushed his eyes with the back of his hand.

Ben squeezed Neil's shoulders. "It doesn't matter. At least you told us now."

"Okay, thanks, son. If you can describe his backpack and the clothes that are missing to the lady constable, that will be a help. In the meantime, we'll search the room for a note or any other clue." The constable straightened. "But Mr. Williams, seems like he's gone off on his own volition, so there may not be much we can do."

"But he's just fifteen!" Ben's voice rose a notch. "Surely that's kidnapping?"

"We'll look at every angle, Sir. I was just letting you know what often happens in cases like these. We'll do our best to locate your son."

Neil was of more help than anyone would have thought. He even knew Jayden's Facebook password.

CHAPTER 27

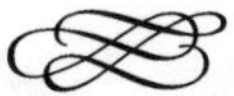

"I'm afraid we'll need to get a Warrant to log into your son's Facebook account, Mr. Williams, and I'm not sure how long that will take." The woman constable levelled her gaze at Ben, and then leaned closer, lowering her voice. "But if you want to log in while we're waiting, that's up to you."

Ben wasted no time. He thanked the Constable and then sat down with Neil and Tessa and logged into Jayden's Facebook account.

They found a litany of chat conversations, most of them to and from Kathryn. She'd dropped Williams from her name and resorted to her maiden name of Middleton.

Ben clicked on her photo and read the latest messages she'd sent to Jayden. They mostly talked of how much she'd missed him and how much she wanted to see him again. No apology or explanation for why she'd left in the first place, but she'd invited him to come and stay with her. She'd sent photos of her

Florida mansion and told Jayden that if he stayed with her he'd be able to travel the world and pretty much do whatever he wanted. There was no mention of Luke Emerson, and Ben couldn't determine if they were still together or not.

The more he read, the more his heart rate increased. He couldn't believe that Jayden had been so deceptive. The last message read, "See you soon, Mum." Ben looked at the time it was sent. Twelve o'clock. Three hours ago. *Not long before Tessa had her fall.*

"We need to check the airport." Ben jumped up as adrenalin flooded his veins, pounding its way through his body. "Neil, stay here with Tessa. I need to go."

Tessa grabbed his hand. "Slow down. Shouldn't we speak with the police first?"

"You can, but I'm going to the airport. There's not a minute to spare."

"I'll speak with them, and I'll pray. Ben... stay safe..." Tessa's voice trailed off as he raced out of the building and sprinted to the car park fifty metres away. The wind knocked him about as he shielded his face from the sleet. As he approached the car, he pressed the beeper. He flung the door open, climbed in and slammed it shut behind him. He inserted the key, and the engine of the rental car roared to life, the wheels spinning on the damp gravel as he sped off. He punched "Airport" into the Navigator and prayed he wouldn't slide on the icy road.

The whole way there he prayed. He prayed he'd get there in time, and that Jayden would have a change of heart. He couldn't believe this was happening. After everything they'd been through together, how could Jayden do this? Jayden knew what Kathryn was like. How could he have been taken in by her empty promises? *God, I give this situation to You. I'm sorry for my reaction earlier, but Lord, I just need to find him.*

FIFTEEN MINUTES AFTER HE LEFT, Ben arrived at the airport. He pulled up in front of Departures, taking no notice of any parking restrictions, and raced into the building. He scanned the Departures board. No direct flight to Florida listed. Only one to New York. Panic set in. He had to think quickly. *What airline would Kathryn fly? And which route would she take? Air New Zealand? Via Hawaii? That would be the one.*

He raced to the Air New Zealand help desk about thirty metres away. A woman with neat dark hair looked up as he came to a sliding halt in front of her. Compared to Ben's frantic state, she appeared cool and calm.

"I'm looking for my son. I think he might be on the flight to Hawaii which is boarding now. My ex-wife's kidnapped him." That wasn't entirely true, but there was no time to explain.

The woman's eyes widened and she met Ben's gaze. "I'm sorry, Sir. We can't give out any passenger details, even if it's your son you're looking for. We'd need instructions from the Police and Immigration to stop the plane."

Ben's heart fell. Tessa had been right. His phone rang in his pocket. *Tessa's ring tone.* "Okay, I'm sorry. Thank you." He stepped away from the counter and drew his phone out of his pocket and answered it.

"Ben." Tessa's voice was barely a whisper. "Kathryn and Jayden left on her private jet half an hour ago."

He went into a tail spin as Tessa's words sunk in. His heart raced dangerously fast and he couldn't breathe. He slumped into a corner, and putting his hands over his head, sobbed until he could sob no more.

Tessa kept talking into the phone hoping Ben would respond. The news she'd just given him had been devastating, and she wished she was with him. Tears spilled down her face and she could barely breathe. But however bad her pain was, Ben's would be a hundred times worse.

He finally uttered a sound of sorts. His voice was so weak she could barely hear him. She'd never heard him so broken.

"Ben, are you okay?" Her voice caught in her throat. She swallowed the lump that was sitting there, pushing it down so she could speak.

"Tess…" Ben's voice trailed away.

"Ben. Wait there. Don't drive. Eversley's on his way to get you."

Silence.

"Ben, did you hear me?"

Seconds passed before Ben mumbled what Tessa assumed was a yes.

When Ben returned to the Lodge with Eversley a short while later, all Tessa wanted to do was wrap her arms around him. She stood on her one good foot and hobbled to him. He clung to her and sobbed into her hair, his tears breaking her heart.

"This isn't your fault." Tessa tried to comfort him. "You've been nothing but a good father to Jayden."

He sucked in a sob. "Then why isn't he here? All those times I confronted him about such trivial matters—"

"Even that was done in love." Tessa kissed his hair. "As long as we have each other and God, we can survive this. There's nothing more we can do except trust God to look after Jayden and bring him back home to us."

A strength Tessa couldn't explain coursed through her body. "We will get through this. With God's help, we'll get through it."

~

Ben, Tessa and Jayden's story continues in...

BOOK 3: "TORMENTED LOVE"

NOTE FROM THE AUTHOR

Hi! It's Juliette here. I hope you've enjoyed the second book in "The True Love Series". Ben, Tessa and Jayden's stories continue in Book 3, "Tormented Love".

Make sure you're on my readers' email list so you don't miss notifications of my new releases! If you haven't joined yet, you can do so at www.julietteduncan.com/subscribe and you'll also receive a free copy of *"HANK AND SARAH - A LOVE STORY"* as a thank you gift for joining.

Enjoyed Tested Love? You can make a big difference...

Help other people find this book by writing a review and telling them why you liked it. Honest reviews of my books help bring them to the attention of other readers just like yourself, and I'd be very grateful if you could spare just five minutes to leave a review (it can be as short as you like).

With gratitude,

Juliette

~

OTHER BOOKS BY JULIETTE DUNCAN

Find all of Juliette Duncan's books on her website:

www.julietteduncan.com/library

True Love Series

Tender Love

Tested Love

Tormented Love

Triumphant Love

Precious Love Series

Forever Cherished

Forever Faithful

Forever His

Water's Edge Series

When I Met You

A barmaid searching for purpose, a youth pastor searching for love

Because of You

When dreams are shattered, can hope be re-found?

With You Beside Me

A doctor on a mission, a young woman wrestling with God, and an illness that touches the entire town.

All I Want is You

A young widow trusting God with her future.

A handsome property developer who could be the answer to her prayers…

It Was Always You

She was in love with her dead sister's boyfriend. He treats her like his kid sister.

My Heart Belongs to You

A jilted romance author and a free-spirited surfer, both searching for something more…

A Sunburned Land Series

A mature-age romance series

Slow Road to Love

A divorced reporter on a remote assignment. An alluring cattleman who captures her heart…

Slow Path to Peace

With their lives stripped bare, can Serena and David find peace?

Slow Ride Home

He's a cowboy who lives his life with abandon. She's spirited and fiercely independent…

Slow Dance at Dusk

A death, a wedding, and a change of plans…

Slow Trek to Triumph

A road trip, a new romance, and a new start…

Christmas at Goddard Downs

A Christmas celebration, an engagement in doubt…

The Shadows Series

A jilted teacher, a charming Irishman, & the chance to escape their pasts & start again.

Lingering Shadows

Facing the Shadows

Beyond the Shadows

Secrets and Sacrifice

A Highland Christmas

A Time For Everything Series

A mature-age Christian Romance series

A Time to Treasure

She lost her husband and misses him dearly. He lost his wife but is ready to move on. Will a chance meeting in a foreign city change their lives forever?

A Time to Care

They've tied the knot, but will their love last the distance?

A Time to Abide

When grief hovers like a cloud, will the sun ever shine again for Wendy?

A Time to Rejoice

He's never forgiven himself for the accident that killed his mother. Can he find forgiveness and true love?

Transformed by Love Christian Romance Series

Because We Loved

Because We Forgave

Because We Dreamed

Because We Believed

Because We Cared

Billionaires with Heart Series

Her Kind-Hearted Billionaire

A reluctant billionaire, a grieving young woman, and the trip *that changes their lives forever...*

Her Generous Billionaire

A grieving billionaire, a devoted solo mother, and a woman determined to sabotage their relationship…

Her Disgraced Billionaire

A billionaire in jail, a nurse who cares, and the challenge that changes their lives forever...

Her Compassionate Billionaire

A widowed billionaire with three young children. A replacement nanny who helps change his life…

The Potter's House Books...

Stories of hope, redemption, and second chances.

The Homecoming

Can she surrender a life of fame and fortune to find true love?

Unchained

Imprisoned by greed — redeemed by love.

Blessings of Love

She's going on mission to help others. He's going to win her heart.

The Hope We Share

Can the Master Potter work in Rachel and Andrew's hearts and give them a second chance at love?

The Love Abounds

Can the Master Potter work in Megan's heart and save her marriage?

Love's Healing Touch

A doctor in need of healing. A nurse in need of love.

Melody of Love

She's fleeing an abusive relationship, he's grieving his wife's death...

Whispers of Hope

He's struggling to accept his new normal. She's losing her patience...

Promise of Peace

She's disillusioned and troubled. He has a secret...

Heroes Of Eastbrooke Christian Suspense Series

Safe in His Arms

SOME SAY HE'S HIDING. HE SAYS HE'S SURVIVING

Under His Watch

HE'LL STOP AT NOTHING TO PROTECT THOSE HE LOVES. NOTHING.

Within His Sight

SHE'LL STOP AT NOTHING TO GET A STORY. HE'LL SCALE THE HIGHEST MOUNTAIN TO RESCUE HER.

Freed by His Love

HE'S DRIVEN AND DETERMINED. SHE'S BROKEN AND SCARED.

Stand Alone Christian Romantic Suspense

Leave Before He Kills You

When his face grew angry, I knew he could murder...

The Madeleine Richards Series

Although the 3 book series is intended mainly for pre-teen/Middle Grade girls, it's been read and enjoyed by people of all ages. Here's what one reader had to say about it: *"Juliette has a fabulous way of bringing her characters to life. Maddy is at typical teenager with authentic views and actions that truly make it feel like you are feeling her pain and angst. You want to enter into her situation and make everything better. Mom and soon to be dad respond to her with love and gentle persuasion while maintaining their faith and trust in Jesus, whom they know, will give them wisdom as they continue on their lives journey. Appropriate for teenage readers but any age can enjoy." Reader*

Connect with Juliette:

Email: juliette@julietteduncan.com

Website: www.julietteduncan.com

Facebook: www.facebook.com/JulietteDuncanAuthor

Twitter: https://twitter.com/Juliette_Duncan

ABOUT THE AUTHOR

Juliette Duncan is a USA Today bestselling author of Christian romance stories that 'touch the heart and soul'. She lives in Brisbane, Australia and writes Christian fiction that encourages a deeper faith in a world that seems to have lost its way. Most of her stories include an element of romance, because who doesn't love a good love story? But the main love story in each of her books is always God's amazing, unconditional love for His wayward children.

Juliette and her husband enjoy spending time with their five adult children, eight grandchildren, and their elderly, long haired dachshund, Chipolata (Chip for short). When not writing, Juliette and her husband love exploring the wonderful world they live in.

Connect with Juliette:

Email: author@julietteduncan.com

Website: www.julietteduncan.com

Facebook: www.facebook.com/JulietteDuncanAuthor

Twitter: https://twitter.com/Juliette_Duncan